B51 096 113 6

KT-237-396

DOUBLE-CROSS

Award-winning books from Sophie McKenzie

GIRL, MISSING

Winner Richard and Judy Best Kids' Books 2007 12+
Winner of the Red House Children's Book Award 2007 12+
Winner of the Manchester Children's Book Award 2008
Winner of the Bolton Children's Book Award
Winner of the Grampian Children's Book Award 2008
Winner of the John Lewis Solihull Book Award 2008
Winner of the Lewisham Children's Book Award
Winner of the 2008 Sakura Medal

SIX STEPS TO A GIRL

Winner of the Manchester Children's Book Award 2009

BLOOD TIES

Overall winner of the Red House Children's Book Award 2009
Winner of the Leeds Book Award 2009 age 11–14 category
Winner of the Spellbinding Award 2009
Winner of the Lancashire Children's Book Award 2009
Winner of the Portsmouth Book Award 2009 (Longer Novel section)
Winner of the Staffordshire Children's Book Award 2009
Winner of the Southern Schools Book Award 2010
Winner of the RED Book Award 2010
Winner of the Warwickshire Secondary Book Award 2010
Winner of the Grampian Children's Book Award 2010
Winner of the North East Teenage Book Award 2010

THE MEDUSA PROJECT: THE SET-UP

Winner of the North-East Book Award 2010
Winner of the Portsmouth Book Award 2010
Winner of the Yorkshire Coast Book Award 2010

SOPHIE ◆ McKENZIE

THE MEDUSA PROJECT
DOUBLE-CROSS

SIMON AND SCHUSTER

With thanks to Moira, Julie, Gaby, Mel, Lou and Lily

First published in Great Britain in 2011 by Simon and Schuster UK Ltd,
a CBS company.

Copyright © 2011 Sophie McKenzie

This book is copyright under the Berne Convention.
No reproduction without permission.
All rights reserved.

The right of Sophie McKenzie to be identified as the author
of this work has been asserted by her in accordance with sections
77 and 78 of the Copyright, Design and Patents Act, 1988.

Simon & Schuster UK Ltd
1st Floor, 222 Gray's Inn Road, London WC1X 8HB

This book is a work of fiction. Names, characters, places
and incidents are either the product of the author's imagination or are
used fictitiously. Any resemblance to actual people living or dead, events or
locales is entirely coincidental.

A CIP catalogue record for this book
is available from the British Library.

ISBN: 978-0-85707-069-2

1 3 5 7 9 10 8 6 4 2

Typeset by Hewer Text UK Ltd, Edinburgh
Printed and bound in Great Britain.

www.simonandschuster.co.uk
www.sophiemckenziebooks.com
www.themedusaproject.co.uk

For Jo, Michele and Pat

ROTHERHAM LIBRARY SERVICE	
B516113	
Bertrams	20/09/2011
JF	£6.99
WIC	

Fourteen years ago, scientist William Fox implanted four babies with the Medusa gene – a gene for psychic abilities. Fox's experiment left a legacy: four teenagers – Nico, Ketty, Ed and Fox's own daughter, Dylan – who have each developed their own distinct and special skill.

Initially, the four worked together as the Medusa Project – a secret, government-funded, crime-fighting force.

But now the teens have discovered that their mentor – and head of the Medusa Project – Geri Paterson has betrayed them.

In fear for their lives, the Medusa teens have run away to France . . .

1: The Journey

I still couldn't get my head around it.

Geri Paterson – the person who'd brought the four of us together as the Medusa Project – had tried to kill me.

Not just me. She'd tried to kill Dylan, too – and would have gone after Ketty and Ed if she'd had the chance.

And now we were running away from her, from home and from England . . .

'Nico.' Ketty's voice beside me brought me back to the reality of the ferry's café where the two of us had just shared a chocolate bar. 'They've just announced we'll be docking in ten minutes; we need to get into position.'

I shook myself. Time to focus.

It was late at night and we were on a ferry bound for Calais in France. Having no ID with us – and not wanting to leave a trail for Geri to follow – we'd sneaked on board using a combination of Ed's hypnosis/mind-reading skills and my telekinetic ability to move stuff with my mind.

So far so good. But getting off without having to go

through any security checks was going to be *much* trickier.

Ed and Dylan raced up and the four of us made our way to the back of the ferry. Outside the wind was fierce, and the salt smell strong in the night air. As the ferry docked, Ketty shivered in her sweats and I put my arm round her.

Her dark curls brushed against my skin. For a second, I wished we could be alone, but I put the thought to the back of my mind. I'd have the chance to spend some time with my girlfriend later.

'So what's the plan?' Dylan snapped, fixing me with her piercing green eyes. She'd been in a bad mood ever since we'd left England. And though she had saved my life last night, my patience with her was wearing thin.

'We hide until everyone's off the boat,' I said, wiping spray off my face. 'Then I teleport you over the sea to that pier over there, one by one.' I pointed across the dark water to a wooden structure a few hundred metres away that reached into the sea. It wasn't a modern pier with buildings and fairy lights strung up for tourists, but old and bleak, with what looked like a small lighthouse at the end.

'Suppose someone sees us?' Ed asked.

'They won't,' I said. Our ferry was moored at the end of a dock, facing out to the ocean. The route across the sea to the pier was dark and unwatched. If I kept the others low over the water, there was no reason why anyone should spot them.

'What about you?' Ketty looked up with concern. 'How will you get off the ferry?'

2

'I'll be fine,' I said. 'It'll be easy to sneak through security if it's just me by myself. Plus, I've got my telekinesis – and if anyone stops me, I'll just talk my way out of trouble.'

'Yeah, you'll be good at that,' Dylan said with a slight sneer to her voice.

I gritted my teeth. I could understand why she was upset. Geri Paterson had tried to kill us yesterday because we'd found out she murdered Dylan's parents when we were all babies.

Still, the news didn't just affect Dylan. Her dad, William Fox, was the scientist who discovered, then copied, the Medusa gene . . . the very person who'd given us all our psychic gifts.

Finding out Geri had killed him – and lied about it – was a big deal for us all. Knowing she was prepared to kill us to keep us quiet was about the biggest deal I could imagine.

The ferry emptied. We waited, still hidden at the back of the boat. After five minutes or so all the other passengers had gone.

'Time to go,' I whispered. 'Ketty, you first. I'm going to teleport you right to the end of the pier, next to that little lighthouse.'

She nodded. 'Don't drop me in the water,' she said with a nervous grin.

I leaned forward and kissed her cheek. 'I won't.'

'Get on with it,' Dylan hissed.

3

Ignoring her, I turned to Ed. 'You need to use your telepathy to keep in constant contact with Ketty while I'm teleporting her, so she can let us know if there's some obstacle I can't see in the darkness.'

'Sure.' Ed swallowed.

'Dylan, you keep watch,' I said.

'Awesome,' Dylan scowled. She crept onto the deck and scanned the ferry. 'I can't see anyone.'

'Good, let's go.' I focused for a second, then lifted Ketty with my mind. She hovered momentarily, just off the deck, tucking herself into a ball so as to be less noticeable.

'This is weird,' she said.

I moved my hand, gesturing in the direction I wanted her body to move . . . over the side of the ferry and down low, to a position just half a metre or so above the sea.

I teleported her slowly and carefully across the dark water. After a few metres she disappeared from view, swallowed up in the night. I kept propelling her towards the pier, trying to keep her body at a steady pace and height over the waves. Ed stood beside me, concentrating intently. He was inside Ketty's mind, our only way of communicating.

'How's Ketty doing?' I whispered.

'Fine, but she says she's a bit too close to the water,' Ed whispered back. 'Her feet are getting wet.'

I lifted my hand, sensing Ketty's body rise slightly into the salty air. I focused on the pier ahead. By my reckoning, Ketty should be over halfway there by now.

4

'There's still no one coming,' Dylan hissed from across the deck, 'but I can hear voices in the distance.'

I gulped. Chances were that someone on the ferry would walk around, checking to see that all the passengers had got off. We had to hurry. I increased the speed at which I was moving Ketty.

'Slow down, Nico,' Ed urged. 'Ketty says she's almost there. Yeah, she's saying stop and lift her up to the pier.'

I visualised Ketty hovering over the water and raised my hand to lift her up telekinetically. Across the sea, the pier loomed in the moonlight. I strained my eyes, trying to catch a glimpse of movement. *There.* A tiny, dark blur at the very end of the pier. It could have been a bird flapping past, or a shadow, but I was certain it was Ketty.

'Right, she's over the pier now,' Ed said. 'Put her down.'

I focused on the dark shape, setting it as close to the ground as I could.

'Okay, you can release her,' said Ed.

I let the telekinesis seep away, watching as the dark shape on the pier unfurled into a human form. As Ketty stood up, Dylan marched over.

'My turn,' she said. 'And for goodness' sake move a bit faster this time.'

I rolled my eyes at her, but said nothing. I glanced across the deck. Neither sight nor sound of anyone else on the ferry, but it was surely only a matter of time before someone appeared.

Dylan swept her long, red hair up into a dark cap and

nodded at me to show she was ready. I teleported her, moving her more quickly than I'd transported Ketty. Ed guided me as he had before. By the time I'd set Dylan down on the pier next to Ketty, I wasn't even having to focus too much on what I was doing. It was funny to think how hard telekinesis once was for me to control. Now I can move whatever I want, within reason.

Not myself though. That's always bugged me, to be honest. I mean, I can teleport everyone else, but I have no idea how to move myself telekinetically from one place to another.

Still, at that point the limitations of my telekinesis were really the last thing on my mind. I had to concentrate. Get Ed onto the pier, then get myself off the ferry.

As I teleported Ed across the water, I heard shouts coming from along the deck. Trying not to lose focus, I ducked behind a funnel. Any second there'd be some-body walking round here, checking there was no one left on board.

It wasn't the deckhands themselves I was worried about . . . but if anyone realised I was here without a ticket or a passport or an accompanying adult, it would only be a matter of time before Geri tracked me down – and that would put us all in terrible danger.

I'm at the pier, Ed thought-spoke. *Set me down.*

I teleported Ed onto the ground. *I reckon it'll take me ten minutes to get round to the pier once I'm through the terminal*, I thought-spoke. *See you then.*

Ed broke the connection. Now I had to focus on getting off the ferry and through the security checks without anyone spotting me. I peered out from behind my funnel. The voices I'd heard before were getting closer. I headed off the deck, back into the ferry. I had to go through the interior to reach the exit to the dock.

I slipped inside the lounge. Two men were coming through a door on the far right. I flattened myself against the wall, heart pounding. Had they seen me?

No, and they weren't coming in my direction either. Though I couldn't see them any more, I could hear their chatter as they crossed the ferry lounge, clearly heading for the café area, which I knew was on the other side of the boat.

As their voices died away, I straightened up from the wall and crept to the next door. Through that, no problem. Then down some stairs to the foot passenger exit. A couple of guys in overalls were visible below me. They were busy ushering the last few cars off the boat and didn't see me.

I did my best to look fairly casual as I sauntered down the side ramp. The passageway to the terminal building was cordoned off. I looked around. There had to be another way off the dock other than through the customs and immigration area.

Yes, there were a series of locked doors opposite, all marked *Staff Only*. Giving a quick glance around to check no one was looking in my direction, I unlocked the first door using my telekinesis. It opened into a storeroom. I shut it and moved to the next one.

Again the door was locked, but it was easy enough to unclick. The room inside was large, like a hanger, and unlit. In the distance I could hear the thump and scrape of boxes being loaded on shelves, but from where I was standing I could see nothing. More importantly, I couldn't be seen myself. I felt my way round the wall until I reached a door. There were voices on the other side of it, so I moved on. A minute or so later I came to another door. I unlocked it and pushed it open. I was on a patch of deserted dock. The night air blasted me, straight off the sea. I climbed onto the railings beside the water and looked around, trying to get my bearings. Ah, there was the terminal building to my left and there were the moored ferries behind.

My spirits soared. If I followed this part of the dock along, I would come to the car exit checkpoint. I could see the row of booths from my railing. There was only one official per booth and streams of cars driving through. Surely I'd be able to slip past unnoticed.

I tiptoed along the railings until I reached a high gate. Through the bars I could see the car exit area. *Mmm*, maybe it was going to be harder to slip past than I thought. The whole area was very brightly lit.

I glanced around. There was another way out – I hadn't noticed it before – to the right of the car exit area. It was a staff entrance consisting of a small barrier, manned by two officials, and not visible from the public areas. Beyond it was the busy road with the town of Calais beyond. As I watched, a couple of dockhands sauntered through, showing their passes to the officials as they did so. I calculated that the distance between me and the exit was no more than a hundred metres or so. Directly beside me was a store area loaded with barrels and boxes. Beyond that, the dock area was full of shadows, but I couldn't see anyone else in the vicinity.

This exit was my best bet for getting out of here. All I had to do was find some way of distracting the officials. Summoning all my courage, I tugged my cap low over my face, shoved my hands in my pockets and strolled towards the exit.

'Eh, hello?' The voice was male and heavy with a French accent.

I spun around, shocked, as a huge man with a tattoo creeping up his neck stepped out of the shadows cast by the barrels. I hadn't seen him. My mouth fell open. What on earth did I do now?

The man spoke again, a torrent of French I didn't understand.

I glanced at the wall behind him. A fire extinguisher hung there. It would be noisy and messy and draw huge attention to myself, but I couldn't see any other option.

'Eh?' The man was getting cross. 'English? What you do here?'

'Nothing,' I said, my heart hammering like a machine gun.

With a subtle twist of my hand, I focused on the fire extinguisher. A second later the lock that held the cylinder in place sprang open and the extinguisher fell to the ground.

I flicked the top off. *Whoosh*. Foam sprayed everywhere. I telekinetically pointed the nozzle right at the man's face. He gasped. Tried to sidestep it. As he slid and tripped, I broke into a run, heading for the exit.

I could hear the foam still spraying everywhere behind me. The officials at the exit were staring at me, open-mouthed.

One raised his hands, turning to the other with a bemused expression. Maybe they were too stunned to react. Maybe I could just hurdle the barrier and run past them before they had time to think.

I pushed myself on, my lungs burning with the effort. Only a few more seconds and I'd be there.

'*Arrêtez-le!*' the man behind me yelled and the two officials at the exit snapped to attention.

I was only metres away. One of the officials drew his gun and pointed it at me. I skidded to a stop. I was panting as he marched towards me. Behind me I could hear the man I'd covered in fire extinguisher foam racing up from behind.

My heart sank. I was totally trapped.

2: A Strange Sight

The man coming up behind me slipped in the fire extinguisher foam and fell to the ground. I focused on the exit ahead and on the two officials who stood between me and freedom.

The one with the gun lowered his arm and said something to his companion. He spoke too fast for me to understand the words, but I caught the word '*jeune*' which I was certain meant 'young' as in . . . 'just a young guy'.

I started running towards the exit. The other official spread out his arms to stop me. '*Arrêtez-vous!*' he yelled. 'Stop!'

I kept my eyes on the man's gun. Out of the corner of my eye I could see officials in the booths looking over at me and car passengers straining to see what was going on.

This was not the discreet exit I'd hoped for.

Making the movement as subtle as I could, I twisted both hands. *Wham*. The two guards fell forwards, smack on the tarmac. I passed them, still running full pelt.

Through the gate and out of the terminal I raced on. I crossed the road and darted down a side street. Then another. I took a few more twisty turns, then finally stopped. I leaned against a lamp post, my lungs burning, taking in huge gulps of air.

I looked up. Listened hard. There was no sound of men chasing me. No raised voices.

I'd lost them.

Still panting, I thought over what had happened. I was sure I couldn't be identified on the CCTV at the terminal – I'd kept my cap pulled low over my face the whole time. And it would seem odd, but not inexplicable, that the two guards I'd teleported might have tripped over and that the fire extinguisher had accidentally fallen off the wall. Hopefully, Geri wouldn't ever hear about it, let alone put two and two together and work out I'd been here, using my telekinesis.

I let out a long, shaky breath and set off again, along the back streets, towards my meeting point with the others. As I did so, Ed appeared in my head, asking where I was. Apparently, the ten minutes I'd allowed to reach the pier were already up.

I decided against a full account of my escape from the terminal and just told him it had taken longer than I'd expected. It actually took me another fifteen minutes to reach the pier. I'd run so far inland and through such winding side streets that I'd kind of lost my bearings.

At last I found the pier, on a fairly quiet road opposite

a small copse of trees. It was virtually deserted, apart from a few food stalls near the entrance.

I spotted Dylan first. She was standing under a street lamp, her dark red hair shining, staring out to sea. Two guys in baggy jeans were eyeing her up, but Dylan seemed oblivious. She's fit. Every guy I knew fancied her, but I'd never seen her show more than a passing interest in anyone – other than Harry, of course. He was the boy we'd met recently – Jack Linden's son – who'd helped Dylan and me get away from Geri.

As I walked towards Dylan, Ed came up to her. The two guys watched him, evidently astonished that someone so geeky-looking should be on speaking terms with anyone as hot as Dylan. And then Ed turned and saw me. He threw his hands up as I approached.

'Are you all right?'

'Yeah, fine. Starving, though,' I said. 'Where's Ketty?'

'Your girlfriend's getting us food from that stall.' Dylan pointed across the pier.

I turned and there she was. My Ketty – the prettiest, coolest girl in the universe – smiling as she walked towards us, her eyes fixed on my face. I smiled back, getting that happy, settled feeling I always have around her.

'I got burgers,' she said, holding up four wrapped packages.

'Thanks.' I took one and watched Ketty as she handed out the others. Did I say how pretty she is? Not striking like Dylan, but softer . . . natural-looking, with curly brown

13

hair and big, golden-brown eyes and a small nose that turns up a little at the end. But despite the delicate features, Ketty's the strongest person I've ever met. Not to mention the most stubborn.

In that moment it struck me that I couldn't bear to lose her.

'I didn't want freakin' cheese on mine,' Dylan complained beside me. 'Or fried onions.'

'That's how they came,' Ketty said with a shrug. 'My French wasn't good enough to understand what he was asking. He spoke too fast – I just said "*oui*" to everything.'

Dylan muttered something under her breath and wandered away, across the pier.

'So what do we do now?' asked Ed.

'We need to contact our families,' Ketty said. 'We've got phones and, now we're off the ferry, there's a signal. I want to call home and let my parents know I'm okay. D'you think it's safe, Nico?'

I glanced around before speaking, to check we were quite alone. To my relief, the two guys who'd been eyeing up Dylan had disappeared and the nearest people, a couple, were crossing the road several metres away. In the distance another ferry was docking at the terminal.

I looked at Ketty and Ed. 'Geri thinks that Dylan and I are dead, so we should both be fine calling home. But right now she thinks you two have gone on the run, so there's a good chance she'll have your home phones tapped in case you call in on them. It doesn't matter. I'll call home and speak to Fergus . . . He can get a message to your families.'

Ketty and Ed nodded their agreement. They both looked pale and strained.

'However, we don't have much time,' I went on. 'The explosion at Wardingham will cover our tracks for a while, but I reckon we've only got a few hours until Geri realises our bodies aren't in that building. Fergus is one of the first people she'll go to and she won't hesitate. She'll be after us with a vengeance.'

Ed looked around nervously.

'Did I hear someone say the word "vengeance"?' Dylan walked over, crumpling her burger wrapper in her hand. 'Because that's the priority as far as I'm concerned. We can't let Geri get away with trying to kill us – or murdering my parents.'

There was an awkward silence. Ketty caught my eye.

'But Geri is so powerful,' she said with a frown. 'I don't see how we or our parents can act against her. I mean, look at us. We've got hardly any money and no useful papers. We don't even have any clothes, other than what we're wearing. And we've got no proof that Geri's done anything wrong. We might be better off just finding somewhere to live outside the UK. We can probably get work somewhere – and our parents will help support us.'

'But even if our parents help, we won't have enough money,' Ed said, clearly aghast. 'And we're too young to get jobs. I mean, we should be at school right now. Anyway, I *want* to take my GCSEs next year . . . I want to do A levels and go to uni and—'

'*Jeez*, I'm sorry us finding out that my parents were murdered is getting in the way of your education, Ed,' Dylan drawled sarcastically.

The atmosphere tensed.

'Man, could you two calm down?' I said. 'We have our psychic abilities. We're more powerful than we think. Anyway, we don't have to decide everything tonight. We just need to find the place Laura booked for us.'

Laura was Harry's mum. She'd helped us get away from England earlier today.

'I checked on my cellphone,' Dylan said. 'The hotel's about a mile away.'

'Good, we'll get going as soon as I call Fergus,' I said.

I was certain Dylan wouldn't have a problem with this. Fergus was her uncle after all – as well as my stepdad and the former head teacher of all of us. However, instead of nodding her agreement, Dylan folded her arms.

'I'm fed up with adults controlling what we do,' she snarled.

'I'm just going to make sure he knows we're okay,' I protested. 'It's the right thing to do.'

Dylan turned away, her face mutinous. Ed sighed again.

'I think Nico's right,' Ketty said quickly. 'We can't let them all worry.'

'Course you think Nico's right,' Dylan muttered. 'You freakin' worship him.'

Ketty rolled her eyes, but said nothing. That's another thing I like about her. Loads of girls would get all huffy or hysterical with Dylan over comments like that, but Ketty doesn't let people get to her. And, even though I knew the past twenty-four hours had been as hard for her as the rest of us – harder, maybe, seeing as she'd been bitten by a guard dog on top of everything else – I also knew that she'd never get all hyper-emotional over stuff that wasn't worth it.

I swallowed the last of my burger. I wanted to make the call to Fergus, but get away from Dylan as well. 'Let's you and me go over there, babe,' I said, pointing to the copse of trees. 'I can call Fergus on my mobile.'

Ketty nodded. We left the pier and crossed the road. There was a path into the trees and, as we strolled towards it, I gazed up at the sky. It was cloudy – the moon hidden behind clouds. And cold. The wind whipped round our heads. I hugged my jacket to me and looked sideways at Ketty. Any other time and I'd have been thinking about taking advantage of the fact that we were on our own. But right now all I really wanted to do was make the call to Fergus.

Ketty was definitely still walking with a slight limp from where the dog had bitten her.

'Does it hurt?' I asked. 'Your leg?'

'Nah, not really.' She paused. 'So where's your phone?'

I grinned. Practical as ever.

I took out my mobile. We'd bought new pay-as-you-go phones on the way to the ferry yesterday, so Geri couldn't trace us. It already seemed like a lifetime ago.

As we reached the little path, I called Fergus on his mobile phone. It went straight to voicemail, so I left a message saying I was fine, but needed to talk to him urgently. I felt better once I'd finished, and pulled Ketty into a huge hug. At least Fergus wouldn't be worrying now. And surely he would call me back soon.

'It's going to be okay,' I said with a grin.

Ketty grinned back. As I bent to kiss her, I caught movement out of the corner of my eye.

I straightened up, on my guard at once. A woman in a dark red suit was in the street just ahead of us. Her sharp blonde bob swished from side to side as she walked, her heels tapping along the pavement. She was looking around for something . . . her face screwed up with anxiety.

'What is it?' Ketty said, turning to follow my gaze.

I pointed at the woman, too shocked to speak. She had stopped to consult a map and was chewing on her lip.

I took a deep breath. 'Tell me that's not . . .'

'*Geri* . . .' Ketty said. She turned to me, wide-eyed. 'How can it be?'

We both stared at the woman. It was definitely Geri . . . the same face . . . the same clothes . . . the same hair . . . except, now I was really staring at her, I could see she wasn't holding herself like Geri. She didn't make the same

18

sharp, birdlike movements or exude Geri's usual poise and confidence.

And I'd never seen Geri Paterson look anywhere near that anxious. At that moment the woman looked up. I ducked behind a tree, tugging Ketty beside me, but it was too late. The woman had seen us.

'Nico?' she squeaked, in a high-pitched girl's voice that was a million miles away from Geri's clipped tones. 'Ketty? Is Ed with you?'

I glanced towards the pier. I could just make out Ed and Dylan, their silhouettes shadowy against the railings. They were looking away from us, out to sea.

'It's a trick,' Ketty said. 'Be careful.'

I flung out my hand and teleported a cardboard box from the pavement up into the air. I steadied it for a split second, then hurled it at the woman's face. She ducked, then stood up.

'Stop it, Nico,' she said.

Again with the high-pitched, girly voice. I frowned.

'I'm not Geri,' the woman said. Her face seemed to alter as she spoke, softening and filling out.

'Yes, you are,' Ketty said, her voice shaking.

'No.' The woman screwed up her face, clearly concentrating hard. 'Look.'

And then, before our eyes, she changed. The sharp blonde bob lengthened and darkened . . . the skin paled and the face plumped out and grew smoother . . . the body shrank and narrowed . . .

19

A girl – about twelve years old – stood on the pavement. She looked at us with terrified eyes. 'Please don't throw things at me again. I came after Ed . . . to find you all . . . I know the hotel's on this street somewhere . . . Don't you remember me?'

I stared at her. She did look vaguely familiar, but I couldn't place her. Beside me, Ketty give a gasp of recognition.

'*Amy?*' she said.

The girl nodded.

'Who's Amy?' I turned to the girl. 'Who on earth are you? And how come . . . how come a minute ago you looked just like Geri Paterson?'

'I'm Ed's sister,' Amy said. 'And I have the Medusa gene, too.'

3: Amy

The sea breeze was cold, but it wasn't the air making me shiver now.

'What d'you mean you've got the Medusa gene?' I grabbed Amy's plump arm, still sure this was some kind of trick. 'What's that got to do with you looking like Geri Paterson?'

Amy's eyes filled with tears. 'I realised a couple of weeks ago,' she said. 'I'd been looking in the mirror and I hated my nose and I'd been wishing and wishing to be able to make it straighter and then one day I realised that it was happening. I mean, I could see . . . actually *see* the nose rearranging itself. So I focused on my mouth and my eyes and . . . my size and I realised I could change all that, too. It's hard to hold it all with your whole body, but I'm getting better at it.'

'You mean you're a *shape-shifter*?' I said.

As I spoke, the moon appeared from behind a cloud illuminating Dylan and Ed across the street. They were still standing by the pier railings, looking out to sea, unaware of Amy's arrival.

Ketty nudged me. 'Remember what Harry told us before we left . . . about the records he'd hacked into that proved William Fox threatened to go to the police if Geri sold the Medusa gene?'

I nodded. It had struck me earlier that if Geri had killed Fox to stop him going to the police, that must have left her free to sell the Medusa gene fifteen years ago. At the time I'd kind of assumed she hadn't done so – after all, the four of us were the only people we knew who had the gene.

But Amy's existence suggested Geri *had* sold the gene.

'How old are you?' I asked.

'Twelve,' Amy answered.

'That proves it,' I said. 'William Fox died three years before you were born. That means he couldn't have implanted the Medusa gene inside you. Which means Geri *must* have sold it to someone else who did.'

'Show us how the shape-shifter thing works, Amy,' said Ketty.

Amy swallowed. 'It's hard when I feel under pressure.'

'I know how you feel.' Ketty grimaced. 'I haven't been able to see into the future for hours. Just do your best.'

'Okay.' Amy frowned, closing her eyes. 'Focus on my nose.'

I looked intently at her nose. There was a little bump halfway down. As I watched, the bump smoothed out.

22

'I can change my hair, too,' Amy said, still squeezing her eyes tight shut.

As she concentrated, her shoulder-length hair shortened into a spiky ginger crop.

My mouth fell open. Ketty sucked in her breath.

'That is *really* cool,' she gasped. 'Can you do animals?'

'Er, no.' Amy looked at me anxiously, her hair and nose returning to normal. 'Just other humans – and I have to study them hard before it works, though it got easier once I got my lenses. Except for the hair. That was always easy. I can do that whenever I want.' She hesitated, gazing intently at me.

I shook my head, amazed. I knew the gene worked with other factors such as personality characteristics to come out differently in different people, but I was used to Ed's mind-reading, Dylan's protective skills and Ketty's precognition. It was hard enough to believe another person with the Medusa gene existed, let alone that, in them, the gene had developed into such an extraordinary ability.

'What are you doing here?' I asked.

'I came looking for Ed,' Amy said. 'He contacted me remotely this afternoon, before you got on that ferry . . . and told me you were all okay and that you guys were running away to France. He didn't want to tell me which ferry terminal you were coming to, but I saw it anyway and I followed on the next ferry.'

'You can mind-read, too?' Ketty said.

'No,' Amy sniffed. 'But Ed was in a bit of a state and

23

he wasn't holding back like he normally does when he goes into your head, so I could see all sorts of superficial stuff he was thinking.'

I rolled my eyes. 'Ed didn't mention he contacted anyone,' I said, remembering the conversation we'd had earlier.

'I don't think he likes reminding people he can do remote telepathy with me,' Amy said. 'Anyway, he just wanted me to tell Mum and Dad that he was okay . . . that he hadn't run off for any bad reason.'

'So why did you come after us?' Ketty asked.

'Because . . . omigosh . . . Geri Paterson turned up soon afterwards and said . . .' Amy stopped, her blue eyes filling with tears again.

'Said that Nico and Dylan had died in that explosion?' Ketty said gently. 'We know, but they're both fine, so—'

'No, it wasn't that.' Amy choked back a sob.

'So what *did* Geri say that made you come after us . . . ?' I said, trying not to sound impatient.

'Geri said that Ed and the rest of you broke into this man's house – Bookman – and murdered him. I came to warn you . . . to help you . . .'

The pavement seemed to shift under my feet. Beside me, Ketty slapped her hand over her open mouth.

'No!' She turned to me, her eyes wide with fear. 'She's blaming us for Bookman's death.'

'She made up this whole story that you resented having your identities covered up, even though she'd only done

24

it to protect you,' Amy explained. 'She said you were taking it out on the person behind the original Medusa Project.'

I stared at her in stunned silence.

Ketty exhaled sharply. 'That's clever,' she said. 'Geri comes clean about the fact that we're really alive in order to frame us and then uses that very fact to tie us to the crime that *she's* committed.'

I groaned. '*Man*, this means all the authorities will think we killed a government agent!'

We stood in silence. I forced myself to think it through.

Bookman was the agent in charge of the original Medusa Project. Last night, Geri killed him – before trying to murder us – and now she was pinning the blame on us.

Ketty had turned away and was pacing up and down. 'This is bad. *Really* bad,' she said. 'It won't just be Geri coming after us now. It'll be the police.'

I nodded. 'We have to get away from here. It's too dangerous to stay.'

'Oh, Nico.' Ketty stared up at me, her face pale. 'What are we going to do?'

I swallowed. 'We don't have a choice – we have to find whoever Geri sold the Medusa gene to fifteen years ago.'

'Why?' Amy looked bewildered.

'Because that person will definitely know that William Fox died around the same time and . . . and most likely they'll know that Geri killed him to stop him going to the police.'

25

'I still don't get it,' Amy said.

'It makes sense.' Ketty nodded. 'We don't have any proof that Geri is framing us for Bookman's murder. It's just our word against hers – and she's got the police on her side, too. But if we can get evidence that Geri killed William Fox, it will help explain why she killed Bookman and is trying to make us look responsible.'

'We have to prove her guilt to prove our innocence,' I said. 'Then we'll be able to go home.' I turned to Ketty. 'Can you remember the name of the person William Fox said Geri was going to sell the gene to?' I asked. 'It was in the records Harry found.'

'No, but Dylan will,' Ketty said.

We walked back to the pier.

'What made you travel disguised as Geri Paterson?' I asked Amy. 'Why not your mum or dad?'

'Omigosh,' Amy said. 'I knew Geri was lying about Ed killing someone so I went to her bag while she was talking to my parents and I stole one of her passports.'

'*One* of them?' I said faintly. I guess I shouldn't have been surprised. Geri Paterson had been a government agent for over twenty years.

'Yeah, she had like three or four and they were all in different names,' Amy gabbled. 'So I picked one and took a picture of Geri herself on my phone without her notic-ing so I could study how she looked. I took some money as well and got taxis and then the ferry. It was really hard when I came out cos I forgot *all* the French I know. I

26

would have changed back to being me earlier, but I was scared people would see me and I thought I'd be safer if I looked older.'

'That was really brave of you,' Ketty said. 'Doing all that to warn your brother.'

Amy blushed, then glanced sideways at me.

'I did it for all of you,' she said.

'Thank you,' I said, wondering why her face was getting even redder.

Ed and Dylan were as astounded to see Amy as we had been. And they were equally dumbfounded by her shape-shifting ability. I could see that underneath his amazement Ed was concerned for his little sister – as well as bemused by her being another recipient of the Medusa gene. Dylan, on the other hand, was contemptuous of Amy's eager-to-please manner and gushing ways. Though I also suspected she was more than a little envious of Amy's ability to change the shape of her face and body at will.

'That's awesome,' Dylan said, rather grudgingly, as Amy modelled her face into a longer, more chiselled look. '*Jeez*, if you worked real hard at it, you might even look pretty.'

Amy frowned anxiously. Ketty patted her on the arm. 'You're fine as you are, Amy. Don't listen to her. She's just missing her boyfriend.'

Dylan scowled at this reference to Harry. He'd seemed a nice guy, though I didn't envy him having Dylan for a girlfriend.

'We need to find the person Geri sold the Medusa gene to,' I said. 'They obviously used it on Amy so—'

'But that doesn't make sense,' Ed said. 'Why would my mum have let anyone put the Medusa gene into *another* baby after she already knew it was going to kill her? I mean, she died when I was four. Less than a year after Amy was born.'

A silence fell on the group. One of the things that binds us is the knowledge that the Medusa gene killed all our mothers.

'I agree it seems strange,' I said. 'But there's no other explanation.'

'Maybe Mum just wanted another child . . .' Amy suggested quietly. 'The Medusa gene had already caused the cancer that was going to kill her. Having it implanted again couldn't make things any worse.'

Ed squeezed his sister's hand sympathetically.

'Anyway, the important thing is that Amy's a clue to whoever bought the Medusa gene code from Geri,' I said. 'Their evidence on Geri will help clear our names.'

'*And* help me get revenge on Geri for my parents,' Dylan snarled. 'It wasn't just my dad she killed, remember? Geri murdered my mom, too. I lost her earlier than you guys lost your moms. Geri's responsible for that.'

Another short pause, then Ed spoke.

'I still don't get it. My dad is really against the Medusa gene. I can't believe he'd have let my mum have it implanted again.' He turned to Amy. 'What did he say to you about how you got the Medusa gene?'

Amy made a face. 'He wouldn't say anything, neither would Sandra . . .' She turned to the rest of us . . . 'That's our stepmum. Dad and Sandra wouldn't even admit I *had* the gene until I changed my appearance in front of them. They don't want me to use my ability, they say it's too dangerous.'

'Idiots,' Dylan said.

'Hey,' Ed protested. 'They're only trying to protect us.'

Dylan glared at him.

I held up my hand to shush her. 'Amy, it's very important you try and remember anything that might be relevant,' I said.

'Okay.' She stared at me under the pier lights, blinking earnestly. 'What might be relevant?'

'Anything about your mum's pregnancy?' I said. 'About your birth?'

Amy hesitated. 'Well, there was something a bit strange.'

Ed reached forwards and took her hand. 'What, Amy?'

Amy glanced at her brother, then at me. 'Sandra, our stepmum,' she explained. 'She said I was a test-tube baby and had a surrogate mum . . . because our real mum was too ill to carry me through the pregnancy . . .'

'You mean that when you were an embryo you were transferred to another woman who *wasn't* your biological mother?' Dylan's mouth fell open.

The atmosphere tightened. Amy nodded.

'Yes, Sandra said it happened at the Norgene Clinic in Norwich, where Mum worked . . . It was a fertility clinic – that's how Mum got involved with the whole Medusa gene thing . . .'

Ed squeezed Amy's hand. 'I'm sorry,' he stammered. 'I didn't know, er . . . .'

Amy shrugged. 'No one knew.' She looked away, gazing across the sea into darkness. 'I've never told anyone . . . no one at school. No friends.'

I thought fast. 'D'you know what the surrogate's name was?'

'I think the surname was Church. Mum and Dad wouldn't tell me anything . . . they said she wasn't important. I did see her name on a letter from the clinic once – just for a second. Her surname was definitely Church. Her first name began with S. I didn't have long enough to read it properly, but it was something like Sally or Susie.'

Dylan's eyes widened. 'Could it have been *Sydney*?'

'Maybe . . .' Amy nodded, her eyes widening. 'Yes, it could definitely have been Sydney.'

'That was the name my dad mentioned in his meeting with Bookman,' Dylan said. 'His exact words were, "If the code goes to Sydney, I go to the police."'

I gazed around at the others. 'That's *it*. Sydney isn't a man – or a last name. It's the first name of Amy's surrogate mum. It all fits.'

'I don't know,' Ed said. 'William Fox said, *If the code goes to Sydney*, not *If the code is implanted in a baby then*

30

transferred to Sydney's womb. It's a big leap when we're not a hundred per cent sure.'

'You're overcomplicating the whole thing,' I said. 'We just have to follow the name Sydney.'

'Nico's right.' Ketty's eyes glittered with excitement. 'It's a great lead.'

Dylan nodded. 'The first step is going to the Norgene Fertility Clinic and digging out Sydney Church's records. There's bound to be some clue there. If we can track her down, we've got a chance of getting the evidence we need against Geri.'

'But suppose this surrogate woman *wasn't* the Sydney William Fox talked about?' Ed protested. 'I mean, I can't believe my parents would have knowingly used the Medusa gene again, especially when it might have killed the woman carrying the baby. Plus, if Geri sold Sydney the Medusa gene, how come she didn't know Amy had Medusa powers?'

'Well, maybe Sydney didn't tell her she'd used the gene on Amy,' Dylan said.

'Still, it's a good point.' Ketty's eyes lost their excited look and her face paled. 'Plus, I have to say I'm not wild about going back to the UK. It's going to be risky and—'

My phone blasted into the mild, early evening air. Ketty jumped. I glanced down.

Fergus calling.

Relief flooded through me as I snatched up the phone. 'Fergus? You got my message.'

'Yes.' His voice was tense . . . urgent. 'Listen very carefully, Nico. Geri put a trace on my phone last night. She's been in touch. She knows that you called me thirty minutes ago.'

No. My mind sped on, thinking through the implications of that. 'Whatever she's told you isn't true,' I said. 'We didn't kill Bookman. Geri did. Just like she killed William Fox.' My breath caught in my throat. I hadn't meant to blurt out the news like that. William was Fergus's brother and, like the rest of us, Fergus had assumed William had died in a traffic accident.

'I know, I know.' Fergus's voice cracked. 'I've spoken to Laura. She told me what you found out . . . about Geri killing William and his wife . . . and Bookman.' He cleared his throat. 'Anyway, never mind about that now. There's no time to lose. Geri's tracked you to France. You need to dump the mobile and get out of there. Fast.'

4: The Norgene Clinic

Fergus's call freaked us all out. Trouble was, everyone had a different idea about where to go now we knew Geri was on our tail. Ketty wanted to disappear into the French countryside while Ed inclined more to Paris, where he said it would be easier for us to get lost in all the crowds.

'No way,' Dylan snapped. 'We should get back to England fast. That gives us our best chance of finding Sydney Church and getting proof that Geri killed my parents.'

'It's true that England is the last place Geri will expect us to go,' I said.

'She'll still be watching all the borders,' Ketty protested.

'And there's no guarantee we'll be able to track down this Sydney Church . . . if that is her real name . . . and less that she'll have enough proof to work against Geri,' Ed added, anxiously rubbing his forehead.

'Well, *I'm* going, even if you two losers stay here,' Dylan said viciously.

'Don't speak to them like that,' I said, annoyed. Why did Dylan always have to be so aggressive?

'Don't start on me,' Dylan snapped. 'This is all your fault anyway. I *said* it was a bad idea to call home. We're already lumbered with Princess Ten Faces over there.' She pointed at Amy, who was standing slightly outside the group, bottom lip trembling, then turned an accusing finger at me. 'If you hadn't phoned Fergus, we'd be safe.'

'It wouldn't have taken long for Geri to find us, whatever we did,' I said, my anger boiling inside me. 'Anyway, there's no point arguing over all that now. Our first priority is to get away from *here*. There's a train station in the town – I passed it while I was getting here. I think we should head to Paris first. Ed's right. It's big and busy there – easier for us to throw Geri off the scent. We can decide how – and how quickly – to trace Sydney Church from there.'

The others nodded their agreement. I turned to Amy. 'Okay with you?'

Amy nodded eagerly. 'Okay, yeah. I mean, that's a brilliant plan.'

'Er, thanks.' I frowned.

Beside me, Ketty suppressed a giggle. Why? I mean, Amy was definitely a bit over the top, but what was so funny?

'Amy isn't coming with us,' Ed said firmly. 'She goes straight back to England on the next ferry.'

'But I came to *help* you.' Amy stuck out her chin. For a fleeting second, she looked just like Ed.

34

'But Mum and Dad will be worried sick,' Ed said.

I hesitated. Ed was right, of course. We also didn't want to be saddled with Amy all the way to Paris. But maybe getting her home gave us an opportunity . . .

'It's better if you go back,' I said to Amy. 'You can be our eyes and ears in England. And Ed can stay in touch with you through remote telepathy.'

Amy nodded reluctantly. 'Okay, Nico.'

I turned to the others. 'I'll make sure she gets onto the ferry okay.'

'I can do that,' Ed protested.

'But if anything goes wrong, I can use my telekinesis,' I said firmly. 'We need to get a bit closer to the terminal first, to make sure we get the right boat. Why don't you three find the station and buy tickets to Paris? I'll join you as soon as I've sorted Amy.'

Ed reluctantly agreed. As Amy and I walked towards the ferry terminal, I chucked my phone into the sea. I didn't like not having it with me, but there was no choice. Now Geri knew the number, she would be able to track it whenever it was used.

My plan firmed up as we walked. Amy was almost skipping beside me, chattering away in my ear. I didn't pay her much attention, just strolled along, my mind completely focused on what I was planning to do. I discreetly juggled a handful of euros using my telekinesis as I walked. Doing so helps me concentrate, though it was weird to think that just a few months ago I couldn't

35

even control the bag of chips I attempted to juggle to impress Ketty.

I stopped about a hundred metres from the ferry terminal building. Now we were closer it was obvious which boat was heading back to England. It was loading up with cars and foot passengers.

'I'll change back to Geri and buy a ticket,' Amy said.

'Okay, just to get through immigration, but once you're on board, you should change into someone else,' I said. 'If Geri knows you stole one of her passports *and* that you're a shape-shifter, she might easily work out that you're travelling using her identity.'

'Dad and Sandra won't have told her about the shape-shifting,' Amy insisted. 'They don't want her to know.'

I shrugged. 'They might do anything if they think it will help find you. Anyway, Geri might have known about you having the Medusa gene from the start.'

Amy frowned. 'I'm sure she doesn't . . . if she did, surely she'd have said something by now?'

I had to admit that was probably true. Nothing I'd ever seen Geri do suggested she thought anyone other than Dylan, Ed, Ketty and myself had Medusa abilities.

Amy set off towards the terminal building and I turned my attention to the next part of my plan: I was going to smuggle myself onto the ferry again and go back to England with Amy.

I hadn't told the others – they would never have agreed – but this way, not only could I make sure Amy got safely home, but I could find the Norgene Clinic on my own and extract the information we needed without putting the others at risk.

The first step was getting on board the ferry. I could, I was sure, have persuaded Amy to buy me a ticket when she purchased her own, but I didn't want there to be any record that I'd travelled, which meant I needed a distraction in order to slip past the guards at the gate. The two men that I'd tripped up before were still there, now busy checking foot passengers as they boarded. Keeping well hidden behind the terminal building wall, I moved closer. Beyond the two guards the cars were loading slowly in pairs.

I lifted my hand and, with a sudden twist, forced one of the two lead cars on the ramp up to the ferry to turn and block the path of the cars behind. Immediately, horns blared out in protest. Both guards turned to see what was happening. I twisted my hand, pushing the car further round. Now it was blocking *both* streams of traffic attempting to board. Two drivers had already got out of their cars. The driver of the car I'd turned was still at the wheel, clearly trying to shift his vehicle.

'I've lost control of the steering!' I could hear him yelling out of the window.

One of the other drivers swore. Another shouted.

The two guards dealing with the foot passengers threw each other a look.

'Get over there,' one said in French.

37

The other nodded. He pulled the barrier gates across to bar any further foot passengers from accessing the ferry and together the two men went over to the car ramp.

This was my chance. In the distance I could see more foot passengers approaching, but right now the entryway was free of people. I raced over to the barrier gates that the guards had shut and locked, undid them with a swift click and slipped inside.

I reached behind me to relock the gates as I walked briskly on-board.

Once safely on deck, I let out a long breath. What a relief. I'd made it. Now I just had to find Amy.

She was still looking like Geri, and sitting in the same café where I'd shared a chocolate bar with Ketty just hours before. Her eyes widened as I walked up.

'Nico!'

I grinned. 'Thought you might like some company for the journey back!'

Amy's chin wobbled. 'Omigosh, thank you,' she said, her eyes filling with tears. 'That's really kind of you. I *was* nervous about going on my own. Ed just contacted me with his mind-reading and I was making out I was fine, but actually, I was feeling *really* shaky about getting all the way home in the dark.'

'Oh . . . oh well, I'm glad I'm here, then.' I cleared my throat, unsure how to respond to all that emotion. 'I'm also going back to search for the information we need at the Norgene Clinic.'

Amy stared at me for a second. It was disconcerting to know she was under Geri's sharp features.

'I can help with that,' she said.

I raised my eyebrows. 'You're going home.'

'That doesn't make sense, Nico.' Amy leaned forward earnestly in her chair. 'I can get us into the clinic by pretending to be a woman wanting information on fertility treatment. Once we're in, you can sneak off and search the files.'

'What about your parents?'

'They don't live that far from the clinic – I'll go there straight after. It'll maybe delay me getting home by an hour or two, that's all.'

I considered this. Ed wouldn't like it, of course, but Amy's suggestion certainly made sense.

'Fine,' I said. 'Here's what I think we should do.'

The Norgene Clinic opened at nine a.m. Amy and I were at the door by five past. Ed had contacted me several times by remote telepathy. He reported that the others were furious I'd gone off on my own, though he was actually grateful I was seeing Amy safely home. Clearly, Amy hadn't told him she was accompanying me to the clinic – and I certainly wasn't going to!

I'd had no problem getting the pair of us off the ferry. First, Amy had transformed herself into another woman

– older and plainer than Geri. It was the weirdest thing – her skin stretching as her face lengthened and her eyes growing narrower, her nose longer and her hair, which had been a sharp blonde bob, thinning to a mousy, middle-aged crop.

She finished and looked at me expectantly. 'I've never done it without a mirror before. How do I look?'

'Fab,' I said with a grin. 'It'll work great.'

We'd just walked out with everyone else, then ducked back before the customs and immigration check. As before, I'd unlocked a storeroom door – this time on the ferry terminal concourse – where we'd hidden until the other passengers had exited.

I'd found a back way out of the terminal through a series of warehouses, most of which were completely deserted. Amy had been nervous throughout, but no problem to deal with.

We'd caught two trains to get here, on each occasion with Amy – still disguised as the older, plainer woman – buying the tickets and me keeping my head down and tugging my cap low over my face.

Throughout all of that I'd stayed remarkably calm. But now I was nervous – our success in the fertility clinic would rely on Amy being able to carry off the cover story I'd given her. I wasn't at all sure she'd manage it.

But Amy proved me wrong within seconds.

'I have to see one of your consultants,' she said, striding up to the reception desk.

The receptionist – a plump, middle-aged lady wearing a horrible pink jacket – glanced from Amy to me.

'This is my son,' Amy lied. 'I had to bring him with me. I *have* to speak to a doctor.'

'I'm afraid you'll have to make an appointment,' the receptionist said.

'It's just a quick query,' Amy pushed on. 'I'm sure the doctor can make time for me. I'm planning an article on local fertility treatments for *The Times* and I want to feature the Norgene as a recommended centre.'

The receptionist studied her carefully. 'I'll speak to Mr Mitchell. He's the senior consultant on duty this morning. Maybe he can give you a few minutes.' She ushered us into the waiting room.

It was formal and silent, full of straight-backed chairs and piles of mags. We were the only people in the room.

'Well, they bought me being your son,' I said quietly as we sat down. 'I'm surprised they think you're old enough.'

Amy giggled. 'I don't know how I'm going to interview this doctor . . . I don't know anything about fertility treatments.'

'If someone comes before I'm back, just ask about the process . . . what he does when someone comes along and wants a baby,' I suggested. 'I'll be back as soon as I can.'

Amy nodded. I took a deep breath and slipped out of the waiting room. The reception area was round the corner to the right. A series of other doors were to my left. I wandered along, glancing at the names on the doors as I passed. The second door was labelled *Admin*. This had to be my best bet for finding records on Sydney Church.

I opened the door a crack and peered round. Six pairs of eyes met mine instantly. Man, the room was packed! Full of women at desks or filing cabinets.

Clearly, I was going to have to be more creative in my approach.

'Fire!' I yelled, rushing into the room. 'There's a fire in one of the offices. Set off the alarm. Get out now!'

5: The Discovery

The women in the office looked startled as I yelled again.

'Fire! You have to get out of here!'

For a second, I thought they were all going to stay in their seats. Then one rose, grabbing her bag and walking out from behind her desk.

'Come on!' she urged the others.

Suddenly they all moved, swarming towards me together. I was surrounded. Questions flew at me.

'Where's the fire?'

'How bad is it?'

'Is anyone hurt?'

'It's in one of the rooms upstairs. I was with my mum and the doctor. We saw the flames,' I said breathlessly. 'They sent me down here. We need to get out, warn everyone else.'

'I'll tell reception – they can sound the fire alarm.' One of the women rushed off. The others followed her, calling in at the other rooms as they went.

I followed them to the end of the corridor then, as they headed round the corner towards the waiting room and reception area, I doubled back to the admin office.

Once inside, I sat at the first computer I came to. The woman who'd been using it hadn't logged out so everything was still up and running.

I scanned quickly through the document files as the fire alarm sounded. Its piercing screech filled the air – and my head. I tried to ignore the noise.

It took a couple of long minutes to find the archive for old patients. They were listed by surname and initial. I typed *Church, S.* into the find box.

There. I raced down the form that flashed onto the screen, desperately trying to pick up the main points.

S. Church . . . surrogate . . . in vitro transfer . . . Mrs O'Brien . . . frozen embryo . . .

I stopped. *Frozen embryo?*

I read the section quickly. It was full of medical jargon I didn't understand, but the gist was clear. The baby, a girl, had been originally conceived through IVF as one of twins – a boy and a girl. While the boy had been implanted in his mother's womb, the girl embryo had been frozen and stored for three years. At this later stage, she had been transferred to a surrogate mother at the request of the natural parents – Mr and Mrs O'Brien. A healthy baby – Amy O'Brien – was born eight months later.

I read the words again, trying to make sense of them. Amy was clearly the baby in the report. With a jolt, I realised that the 'twin' referred to must be *Ed*. He'd never mentioned being an IVF baby, but maybe he hadn't known. Anyway, like me, he was three years older than Amy – the dates fitted.

I frowned. All this meant that Amy must have been implanted with the Medusa gene at the same time as Ed. Which meant William Fox had been responsible, not the person to whom Geri later sold the gene code . . . not 'Sydney'.

Heart sinking, I raced to the bottom of the page where the surrogate mother's name was clearly spelled out: Susie Church.

Susie. Not Sydney. Sydney Church did not exist.

I sat back, staring at the screen, the fire alarm still piercing through my head.

I'd followed a complete red herring. Amy's birth had nothing to do with the sale of the Medusa gene.

For a moment, the disappointment overwhelmed me. Then I sat forward again. While I was here, I might as well see if the clinic held any information about William Fox. I went to the main network docs folder and searched his name.

It came up straight away in an article dated the year before I – and the other Medusa teens – was born. William Fox had worked here as a consultant. I flicked down the list of other consultants, making a mental note of their names. Each name was logged next to the consultant's place of work. One in particular caught my eye: *Professor Avery Jones, psychologist, Sydney, Australia.*

Was *this* the *Sydney* William Fox had been referring to in his conversation about the sale of the Medusa gene? It looked as if Jones and Fox had some serious disagreements over the clinic's policies in genetic experiments.

Before I could search any further, the fire alarm stopped and a hefty security guard flung open the admin office door.

'Oy!' he shouted. 'What the hell d'you think you're doing?'

Switching the computer off, I leaped to my feet. The security guard advanced, arms outstretched.

I leaped backwards. The guard reached the desk at which I'd been sitting. Instinctively, I raised my hands and deployed my telekinesis. I rammed the desk into him, then spun it sideways so it shoved against his legs.

The guard stumbled, lost his footing. With a yell, he fell over.

Heart thundering in my ears, I sped past him and raced outside the building. Amy was in a huddle of people at the end of the clinic's driveway.

Everyone stared at me as I flew towards them. They were all talking at once. I caught snatches as I ran up.

'He's the one . . .'

'Said the fire was upstairs . . .'

'. . . set off the alarm . . .'

Amy was standing in the middle of the group, eyes wide and mouth open. I grabbed her arm and dragged her away.

'Hey, come back!'

'Stop!'

The staff's cries echoed after us, but I ignored them, focusing only on putting as much distance between us and the clinic as possible. Amy was panting beside me, clearly struggling to keep up.

I pounded along a tree-lined avenue, then took the left and two rights back to the station. I raced through the open door and stood, panting, in the entrance hall, gazing up at the screens.

There was a train to London in five minutes. 'I'm getting on that,' I said, pointing up to the announcements board. 'You need to get a cab outside to your parents' place.'

Amy stared at me, still gulping in lungfuls of air. She'd changed back to herself as we'd run – though I hadn't noticed until this moment. Her bottom lip wobbled.

'Go home?' she said.

'Yes,' I said impatiently, glancing again at the board. 'I'm sorry I can't take you right to the door, but I need to get out of this area fast.'

'I knew it was you setting off the fire alarm. Omigosh, why didn't you say you were going to?'

'It just . . . I had to think quickly . . .' I explained. 'It wasn't planned.'

'What did you find out in there?' she said.

'That your surrogate mum wasn't the Sydney we're looking for and . . .' I hesitated, then explained what I'd learned about Ed and Amy being IVF twins.

Amy's eyes rounded as I spoke. 'Omigosh,' she breathed. 'So I'm really three years older than I thought.'

47

'I don't think it works like that.' I frowned. 'A frozen embryo doesn't grow, does it? So it isn't exactly alive.'

Amy nodded. 'But if William Fox put the gene in me at the same time as Ed, how come Geri didn't know about it? And how come the surrogate who was carrying me three years later didn't die like my mum did?'

'I don't know. For all you know she did die.' I took a deep breath, trying to keep my nerves under control. I badly wanted to find the platform my train was leaving from. It would be here in just a couple of minutes. 'I'm sorry, but I really have to go.' I said. 'Are you okay?'

'Sure.' Amy swallowed. 'It's just . . . I don't want to be left out . . . I want to help . . . I want to stay with you . . .' She smiled – a sweet, timid smile. For the first time I noticed there was a dimple in her cheek.

I grinned at her. Maybe a bit of flattery would do the trick. 'You look cute when you smile.'

She blushed crimson and lowered her eyes.

'It's not that we don't want you with us,' I said, patting her arm. 'But it'll be really useful to have you back here. Ed can communicate with you telepathically so you can let us know what's going on – I mean, I'd love you to come, but your parents will worry and Ed . . . well, he'd never forgive me if I showed up in France with you again.'

Amy looked up, her eyes all warm and glowy. 'You'd love me to come?'

I glanced at the announcements board again. My train

48

was due in any second. 'Of course,' I said. 'But you'll get me in terrible trouble if you don't go home now.'

'Okay,' she nodded.

'You're a star.' Relieved, I reached forward, pecked her on the cheek and rushed away.

The London train was pulling in as I reached the platform. I scrambled on board and flung myself into a seat by the window. As we pulled away, I caught sight of Amy standing at the fence beside the taxi rank, scanning the carriages.

I waved, but she didn't see me.

I sat back in my seat and let out a long, shuddering sigh. That had been close.

Too close. But maybe my risky search in the clinic's admin office had thrown up the information we needed.

Maybe our Sydney was a place – not a person – and maybe Professor Avery Jones was our next, vital clue.

6: Sydney

It turned out that the article I'd found wasn't the first place that Professor Jones had publicly disagreed with William Fox. According to Ed, who did the research online, they'd been engaged in a long-running feud over several years.

It took a while to discover this, however, as most of the next three telepathic sessions I had with Ed involved him berating me for taking Amy (now safely back at home) to the clinic and drawing so much attention to myself while I was there.

The third exchange took place just as I drew into Liverpool Street Station in London.

Why did you go to the clinic anyway? It's so typical of you to go off on your own like that. I bet you didn't find out anything useful either . . . I mean, if the Sydney who Geri sold the Medusa code to has nothing to do with Amy's surrogate mother, then . . .

And on and on he ranted.

I waited until he was finished – well, there isn't much

choice when Ed's inside your head – then told him what I'd found out about him and Amy originally being IVF twins.

That shocked him. His voice in my head went completely silent and, when he spoke again, his tone was sadder and calmer.

So, if we were originally twins, Amy was conceived at the same time as me, which means this Sydney person can't have been responsible.

I acknowledged that this was the conclusion I'd already come to and told him about the existence of Avery Jones in Sydney. Ed went straight off to investigate, making contact with me half an hour later.

Okay, we've done some research on Professor Avery Jones, Ed thought-spoke. *He's still practising as a psychologist and he still lives in Sydney, Australia, but get this . . . He stopped all his consultancy work at fertility clinics within a few months of William Fox dying.*

Just after the point when Geri must have sold him the Medusa gene code, I thought-spoke.

Exactly. And there's more. Avery Jones knew about Medusa. We found a blog he wrote saying that he knew William Fox was working on a synthetic biology project involving mutant genetics. It was published the week before Fox died – and it actually uses the Medusa name. It hints that Jones wanted the gene and *that he was on the verge of finding out a load more about it. But he never wrote about it again.*

We have to go to Sydney to find him, I thought-spoke. I expected Ed to begin ranting at me again, but to my surprise he agreed.

I know. We've already been onto Laura. She's going to help.

Laura was Harry's mum and Dylan's godmother . . . She knew all about our history and had already put herself in danger to help us escape England on the ferry to France.

How can Laura help us get to Sydney?

Well, firstly, Geri doesn't know we've been in touch with her, so there's no trace on her phone. Secondly, Laura's got someone who's agreed to fly you in secret to Helsinki and arrange for us to meet you there.

What about when we get there?

Laura's managed to get in touch with all our parents. They know Geri's watching them, but they've smuggled our original passports – you know the ones from before Geri gave us new identities – down to her. She's going to give them to you – plus four tickets from Helsinki to Sydney.

What if Geri traces us?

It's a risk, but she's likely to be focusing on airports in England and France.

This was true, though not entirely reassuring.

Three hours later, fortified by a chicken sandwich at Victoria Station, I arrived at the small town of Bixbury in Kent, where Laura was going to pick me up and explain the details of the plan.

It was early afternoon and the sun was high in the sky, beating down on my head through the still air. This had to be the hottest day of the year so far. As I waited outside deserted Bixbury Station, my thoughts drifted to Ketty. Ed hadn't mentioned her earlier – and I didn't have a phone to call her with. Those thoughts led to others and it was with a jolt that I realised Laura was driving up beside me in a green Mondeo.

Slim, suited and with her highlighted blonde hair pulled back in a ponytail, she poked her head out through the open window and offered me a brief, anxious smile.

'Get in.'

'Where's Harry?' I asked, sliding into the passenger seat.

'At school.' Laura drove off, her lips pressed tightly together. 'Which is where you guys should be, too.'

I turned and looked out of the window. Bixbury was one of those typical English towns – all brick houses and roses in the front garden. I didn't need Laura telling me what we should and shouldn't be doing.

'School isn't exactly an option right now,' I said curtly. 'What with Fox Academy being blown up and the government agent supposed to be protecting us trying to frame us for murder.'

'I know.' Laura sighed. 'I just can't believe what that woman – Geri Paterson – is doing . . . making you fugitives . . .'

'So where's this plane?' I said.

'Couple of miles away,' Laura explained, peering at a

road sign through the windscreen. She nodded to a package on the dashboard. 'There are all your passports and tickets. There's a note from Fergus, too, plus contact details for my friend, Sam Hastings, who lives in Sydney. We emailed yesterday and he's going to meet you off the plane in Sydney and look after you until Fergus can get out there.'

Well, that was a relief. But I couldn't help but wonder if we'd make it as far as Sydney.

'This pilot who's taking me to Helsinki in his private plane,' I said. 'Is he for real? I mean, he's going to be breaking about ten laws just smuggling me out of the country.'

'All your parents are covering his payment, Nico.' Laura hesitated. 'I wish I could come with you, but you'll be safe once you get to Sydney and I can't just walk out on work without raising suspicions. Fergus says he's going to fly out to join you as soon as he can give Geri the slip.'

I nodded, opening Fergus's note. It was fairly emotional – at least for Fergus. He wrote about how much I meant to him and ended by urging me to think before I acted, keep my wits about me and look after myself.

I sat back when I'd finished reading, my own feelings a mix of anxiety about what I was about to do and reassurance that at least Fergus and Laura were behind us.

Laura gazed out at the open countryside ahead and smiled. 'Harry's quite taken with Dylan, you know.'

I grinned, pleased to be lifted out of my own thoughts.

'Yeah, I got the impression that it's mutual,' I said,

remembering how flustered Dylan had seemed around Harry.

'What's she really like?' Laura asked. 'I don't mean to pry, but her mother was one of my best friends . . . and I've only spent a few hours with her . . .'

What did I say to that? 'Well . . . Dylan's moody . . . but she's loyal . . .' I started, then stopped, unable to think of anything else to say that didn't have 'pain in the ass' at the end of the sentence. Laura shot me a quick glance, then moved on.

'It's funny, it seems like yesterday we were all together with our babies – Jack and me, and Dylan's mum and dad.' She smiled sadly at me. 'I knew *your* mum, too, Nico. And Fergus. I mean, they were on the periphery of our group, but I met them several times.'

I nodded, feeling awkward. I wasn't used to meeting people who'd known my mum. A photo that Dylan had shown me recently popped into my head. It was of her and Harry, Laura's son, as babies. My mum's in the background of the picture, heavily pregnant. When I saw it, I thought how weird it was that I'd been inside her then. I had that same feeling now, being with someone who'd known her at that time.

Laura turned her eyes back to the road. 'Your mother was beautiful, Nico. Very young and very fragile-looking with big, brown eyes. Fergus used to pad around her like a protective bear or something.' She laughed.

I didn't know what to say. I knew so little about my

mum's life before she met Fergus. She was Italian – a student over here to learn English – who got pregnant, then met Fergus and his brother, William Fox. It was William who, unbeknown to either my mum or Fergus, had injected her with the Medusa gene that created my powers – and killed her.

For the first time it struck me that Fergus must have felt unbearably guilty about that. He loved my mum – and yet it was because of his brother that she'd died.

'Your mother never spoke to me about your birth dad. I know nothing about him and she certainly never said who he was,' Laura went on. 'To be honest, from what Fergus let slip at the time, I don't think she talked about him with anyone.'

I nodded. I was used to not knowing.

A few minutes later we arrived at the airfield. The pilot was eager to set off so Laura assured me again that I'd meet up with the others in Helsinki and went back to her car.

The journey to Sydney was long but uneventful. Despite all my anxieties, I loved the first part of the trip – by myself, on the small plane to Helsinki. The flight stayed low, like the helicopters I'd ridden in twice before – once when Ed and I had sneaked on board a commercial ride to follow Ketty from London to Devon and once flying over the desert in Spain a few weeks ago. However, I'd been hiding under a jacket the first time and unconscious the second, so this was my first real experience of what the landscape looks like when you're a little way above ground.

The others arrived in Helsinki just a few hours after me and we found the main airport easily enough. Once on the jumbo jet to Sydney, we kept ourselves to ourselves for most of the journey. Dylan, as usual, had jammed on her headphones and was listening to that fast dance music she likes so much. Ed spent most of the long journey looking like he was trying not to be sick. Ketty and I talked for a bit, then she said she was going to try and have a vision of the future and spent most of the rest of the journey with her eyes focused on the middle distance. I didn't disturb her. I know she gets stressed out when she loses control of her gift . . . It certainly seems a lot harder to manage than any of the others.

Ed had done a little more research on Avery Jones. We hadn't yet found either a home or work address for him, but I was sure all the details would prove easier to locate once we'd arrived and made contact with Laura's friend.

Dylan made a few digs at me for going off on my own to the clinic without saying anything . . . and for forgetting to take the Clusterchaos software program that Harry had left us. It was a hacker's program – useful, to be sure, though if I was honest, I didn't really understand how to use it. Not that I was going to admit it.

'You could have hacked into the clinic files with Clusterchaos,' she said contemptuously. 'Ed's shown me how to use it; it's real simple.'

'I knew I wouldn't need it,' I lied.

'Oh yeah, I forgot. You know everything,' Dylan snapped.

I ignored this. Dylan was often rude. There was no point taking it personally. The next minute she was asking if Laura had said anything about Harry. She was trying to hide her interest, but it was obvious.

I pointed this out to Ketty, hoping to make her laugh, but Ketty still seemed preoccupied with trying to have a vision of the future so I went back to the in-flight movie selection.

We all fell asleep during the last few hours of the flight. When I woke, it was dawn and we were coming in low over a large forest. Huge, blue-tinged hills were visible in the misty distance.

'Those must be the Blue Mountains,' Ed said. 'They're just outside Sydney.'

We were met at the airport by Laura's friend, Sam Hastings, a smiling, ruddy-cheeked man with a paunch. He chatted to me about Laura while we walked to his car, going into a long, convoluted tale about when they were students over twenty years ago.

I listened politely, then asked how soon we could start tracking down Avery Jones.

'We can talk about that when we get home, sport,' Hastings said. 'When you've had a chance to eat and rest.'

We drove for over an hour, quickly leaving the built-up area near the airport and making our way through miles of dusty scrubland. The air was still and warm – though not as burning hot as I was expecting.

I couldn't get over how huge everything seemed – from the endless stretches of orange-brown earth to the flat green of the trees and bushes that punctuated the landscape, to the mountains that loomed, still misted at the peaks, in the distance.

Hastings finally stopped the car on a long, flat road. He pointed to a corrugated iron hut about fifty metres away.

'Dunny stop,' he said brightly.

We stared at him blankly.

'Bathroom break,' he explained with a chuckle. 'Go on. It's another hour till my ranch. You should stretch your legs.'

The four of us got out of the car and wandered over to the hut. It looked far too run-down to be a proper toilet. I glanced around uneasily, but there was no sign of anyone else for miles.

I followed the others into the hut. It was airless and empty, with a row of cubicles at one end and a grubby towel on the floor next to a large, green door.

'It's unisex,' Ed said, sounding horrified.

'And filthy,' Dylan added.

Ketty and I exchanged amused looks.

'It's not that bad,' Ketty started. 'Why don't . . . ?'

As she spoke, a man and a boy emerged through the green door. The man was unsmiling, with cropped hair and sunglasses and biceps that bulged under his T-shirt. The boy looked a bit younger than me, but was the same height. He was lean and cool-looking – in jeans and a loosely buttoned shirt – with a shock of wild, white-blond hair.

Ketty and I caught each other's eye again. This time Ketty's expression was wary.

The boy grinned as he took us in. 'Hey,' he said in a broad Aussie accent. 'Nico, Ed, Ketty and Dylan?' He looked along the row of us as he spoke, fitting each name to the right person.

I took a step backwards, my heart hammering at my ribs. I tensed myself, ready to perform whatever telekinesis I needed.

'How do you know our names?' I said.

'I'm Cal,' the boy said, ignoring me. 'How was your flight?'

I glanced around. The grubby towel was the only movable item in the hut. I could fling it at Cal's face, but we'd have to run like mad to make it back to Hastings' car before he or the henchman caught up with us.

'What is this, a trap?' Dylan snarled.

'Let's go,' Ed urged.

'You're too late. The man who brought you here's already gone,' Cal said.

I raced to the door, my heart beating fast. Sure enough, Sam Hastings' car was disappearing into the distance.

'What going on?' I demanded. 'Who are you?'

'I'm surprised you're so shocked.' Cal's pale grey eyes rested on Ketty. 'Didn't *you* know we'd be here?'

Ketty shook her head. With a jolt, I realised that he understood about our Medusa gifts. He *knew* Ketty could see into the future. He was asking if she'd seen this moment.

I raised my hands and lifted the towel off the ground. The henchman clocked the movement immediately. His fists clenched and he nudged Cal.

'What do you want?' I said to Cal, trying to keep my breathing steady and my focus on the towel.

The smile fell from Cal's face.

'Don't be an idiot, Nico,' he said in his broad Aussie drawl. 'I told you, we came to meet you. Who do you think sorted out your lift here?'

I caught Ketty's eye. She looked scared.

'A man called Sam Hastings,' I said. 'He . . . he's a friend of a friend. He met us at the airport earlier.'

Cal snorted. 'Didn't you see through that?' he said. 'We intercepted your friend Laura's emails and replied *as if* from Sam Hastings. But the real Hastings himself has no idea you're here. In fact, he's on a bizzy trip to the Far East at the moment. He's not even in the country.'

I froze. I glanced at the others, reading the same alarm in their expressions that I knew was in my own.

I let fall the towel I'd teleported. The henchman followed its movement to the ground, then fixed his eyes on me, clearly tensed in anticipation of my next telekinetic move.

Dylan folded her arms. I was sure she had her force field primed ready to protect herself – and us – if need be. 'So,

61

if Sam Hastings didn't bring us here, who was that man who met us at the airport?'

'An actor we hired for the day,' Cal explained. 'We gave him a bit of info about Laura Linden and descriptions of you pommies and told him to bring you to the meet here.'

The four of us stood in stunned silence.

A few moments passed. I looked from Cal to the man beside him who, I realised with a sinking heart, had the absolute look of a bodyguard about him.

'So who's behind all this?' I asked, my throat dry.

Cal rolled his eyes. 'Isn't it obvious?' he said. 'It's Avery Jones.'

7: The Demonstration

I stood in the middle of the hut, my head spinning. Avery Jones *knew* we were coming.

'How did—?'

'Can we save the quessies?' Cal said impatiently. 'It's just your plane was later than we were expecting and Avery's waiting.'

'Waiting where?' Dylan asked suspiciously.

'His ranch.' Cal smiled at her. His tone was suddenly smooth and charming, completely different from when he'd been talking to me.

'Why does he want to see us?' Dylan scowled at Cal as she spoke.

I was pleased to see that his smarmy tone had made absolutely no impact on her.

Cal shrugged. 'You're original Medusa,' he said. 'Avery's fascinated.'

I stared at him. '*Original* Medusa,' I said. 'Does that mean there are others?'

'Of course,' said Cal contemptuously.

'Who?' Ketty said.

'How many?' asked Dylan.

'Avery will explain when we get home,' Cal said. There was a finality in his voice that made it clear he wasn't going to say more.

A taut silence descended. I could feel the tension building.

'Er . . . would you . . . I mean, you obviously know what we can do . . .' Ed stammered. 'Er . . . so would you let me mind-read you? So we can feel safe.'

'No worries.' Cal glanced at the man in sunglasses beside him.

The guy patted his jacket, revealing the outline of a gun.

My heart thudded.

'So how does this work exactly?' Cal asked.

'Just let me look in your eyes,' Ed said.

As Ed peered into Cal's pale grey eyes, I reached for Ketty's hand and squeezed it. She gave it a quick squeeze back, but kept her gaze on the others.

After a few seconds Ed broke the connection.

'Cal's telling the truth. I didn't go in deep, but Avery Jones is nearby and is expecting us.'

'Ripper,' Cal said briskly. He glanced at me again, his expression hardening. 'Can we go now?'

Suddenly Ed was in my head.

He's telling the truth about Avery Jones and I don't think he's hiding anything, but there's something reckless about him. Be careful.

Sure, tell the girls.

Ed's presence vanished from my mind. I nodded at Cal. 'How do we get to this ranch, then?'

'We brought the car. It's out back,' Cal said.

He led the way past the toilet cubicles to the green door at the back of the hut. The man with the gun and the bulging muscles hung back, waiting for us all to leave. He still hadn't said a word. I stared at him.

'You waiting to take a dump once we're gone?' I asked.

Ketty poked my ribs. 'Don't, Nico,' she hissed.

The man raised his eyebrows, then patted the gun in his breast pocket again. He jerked his head, ordering us through the door.

Outside the sun was blisteringly hot. Beyond the hut the dusty scrubland stretched as far as the eye could see. A sleek, black vintage Bentley was parked outside, hidden from the road by the hut. We walked towards it.

Ahead of me, Ed and Dylan were speaking in low, urgent voices. Cal strolled next to Ketty. He was obviously saying something, though I couldn't hear what. Ketty was looking up at him, her golden-brown eyes wide with amazement.

I hurried forwards, intending to listen, too, but before I reached them, Cal stopped. He pointed along the orange-earth ground to the shining Bentley. My mouth fell open. I hadn't looked properly before but, close to, I could see that the car was absolutely beautiful, especially set against this bleak and dusty landscape.

'Avery sent his car for you,' Cal said, clearly enjoying the look of surprise on our faces. 'Unfortunately, we can't all fit inside. Four passengers only, and there's five of us.'

I frowned. What was he suggesting? I suddenly wondered if Cal and the driver were planning on getting rid of one of us before we set off. I raised my hands instinctively, ready to use my telekinesis, and glanced at Dylan. She was the only one of us who could protect herself – and others – from a bullet. She'd saved my life just two days ago – managing to extend her own protective powers so that they shielded me and Harry from a gas explosion that would otherwise have killed us.

But Dylan hadn't noticed me. She was staring at Cal. 'So, if we can't all fit into the car, how are we all gonna get to the ranch?' she asked.

'Yeah, great plan, Cal,' I said, trying to sound as withering as possible.

Cal laughed. 'I can use my Medusa gift.'

I swallowed. Cal had the Medusa gene? I guessed it made sense. If Avery Jones had purchased the Medusa gene immediately after William Fox's death, then Cal looked about the right age – a year or so younger than me, which . . .

'How exactly does it work?' Ketty's eyes shone as she spoke.

Jealous irritation flickered through me. Ketty didn't sound at all thrown by the discovery that Cal had the Medusa gene. Was that what he'd been talking to her about?

Cal smiled at her, his eyes full of mischief. 'I wasn't supposed to talk about it until Avery had met you, but . . . why don't I show you, Ketty? I mean, it's not like there's anyone watching. This place is deserted.'

No. I opened my mouth to protest, but it was too late.

'What do I have to do?' Ketty asked.

'Nothing, just hold my hand,' said Cal.

What? I stared at Ketty. Surely she couldn't go along with this! Whatever Cal was up to it was an unknown. It was dangerous.

Cal flashed a quick, triumphant look at me. 'See you guys later,' he said. Then, before I could do or say another word, he grabbed Ketty's hand, flexed his knees and zoomed into the sky, pulling Ketty behind him.

My mouth fell open. Cal's Medusa gift was flying?

How on earth did that work?

I stared after the two figures. They both had their legs together and their arms by their sides. As I watched, they separated slightly. Cal steadily extended one arm, then a leg. Beside him Ketty, wobbling in the air, copied his movement. At first, I was swallowed up by terror. Suppose she fell? Suppose Cal's ability stopped working? My own gift had been sketchy at first, after all. But as the moments passed, it was obvious that Cal was a master at what he was doing and, even at this distance, Ketty was clearly enjoying herself. She repeated the moves Cal demonstrated a few more times, getting steadier with each go.

My fears subsided and fury rose up to take their place. How *dare* Cal just leave with Ketty like that? And what was *she* thinking, going along with him so willingly?

'How is he doing that?' Dylan said beside me.

She was staring into the sky, shielding her eyes from the sun, her mouth open in amazement. My rage grew. Ed met my gaze. He looked panic-stricken.

'Did you know Cal could fly?' I demanded.

'I had an idea. I mean, I didn't spend enough time in his head to see exactly, but . . . I think he's kind of got the reverse of your gift. I hope Ketty's okay.'

'What d'you mean, "the reverse"?' I said.

'You can move anything, but not yourself,' Ed explained. 'Cal's the other way round. He can move through space – like people levitate, only with more control – but he can't perform telekinesis.'

'Who needs telekinesis when you can fly?' Dylan said. She was still staring up at the tiny figures in the sky above us. They were performing somersaults now – Cal's neat and elegant, Ketty's slightly more ragged. 'That is the most awesome thing I've ever seen. I have to try it out.'

'It looks really dangerous to me,' Ed said.

I shook my head, suddenly afraid for Ketty again. Suppose Cal let go of her hand? Suppose, in showing off to impress her, he made a mistake?

'Is he safe doing that?' I asked the sunglass-wearing muscleman who was now standing by the open passenger door of the Bentley, waiting patiently to drive us to Avery Jones.

Muscles nodded. He pointed to the inside of the car.

I looked back up at Ketty. I couldn't really tell from here, but it looked as if she and Cal were laughing. A poisonous shot of jealousy pierced through me. As I watched, Ketty put her arms to her sides again, one hand still tightly in Cal's. A second later the two of them had zoomed off, out of sight.

A million emotions churning inside me, I got into the car. It was cool – there was some serious air con going on in here – and smelled of leather. Any other time I would have enjoyed riding in such a smart car, but right then, all I could think about was what Ketty was doing. Was she even the tiniest bit scared? She'd looked happy and excited.

I didn't want to face it, but in my heart that was slicing me up the most: Ketty was loving it up in the skies.

Loving it way too much.

We drove in silence. Dylan asked the chauffeur a few questions, but he didn't answer. Ed announced he'd made remote contact with Ketty.

'She says she's fine. She's safe and having fun.'

'Great,' I snarled.

Ed tried to make remote telepathic contact with me after that, but I told him to 'get lost' – only less politely.

After that he and Dylan resumed the quiet chat they'd

been having earlier. I couldn't hear what they were saying and I didn't care. I was furious with Ketty. Going off like that, not even looking at me before she sped off with Cal. It was humiliating.

As for Cal, I hated him.

I fumed in silence for the rest of the journey. The landscape didn't change for twenty minutes – just endless, orangey-brown scrubland, leading to distant, olive-green forests and blue-tinged hills. Then, as we rounded a bend in the dirt track we were driving along, the outline of a low-rise town rose up ahead.

The driver pulled over and stopped the car.

'What's going on?' I said.

He pointed out of the window. Cal and Ketty were gently coming in to land beside us. Ketty's face was flushed, her hair all messed up and her eyes were glittering with excitement. She looked as pretty as I'd ever seen her. Cal landed lightly on his toes, catching Ketty round the waist as she stumbled.

She laughed. So did he.

I wanted to hit something.

Ketty raced over to the car. She yanked the back door open and scrambled in.

'That was *amazing*!' she said, glancing around at us.

'How does it work?' Dylan asked, shifting sideways to make room for her. It struck me that, normally, Dylan would have made some sarky comment about having to move over.

70

'It feels really weird when you start,' Ketty gabbled excitedly. 'Kind of disorienting. But Cal was really calm and when I did what he said, I realised that if I trusted him to hold me up, I was free to move my body much more than I thought. There are wind pockets that catch you, too.'

'It looked *sooo* awesome.' Dylan peered past Ketty, to where Cal was now taking off his T-shirt and tying it round his waist.

My mouth fell open for the second time that hour. Cal might be younger than me, but he was incredibly toned – with curving arm muscles and a six-pack.

'He is *ripped*,' Dylan said. 'Would he take me up?'

She and Ketty started giggling.

I gritted my teeth.

'Sure,' Ketty said. 'We came down because Cal wants to run the rest of the way to the ranch. He's really into running, just like me. He's going to show me the best tracks round here later.'

Oh, great.

With a brief wave at the car, Cal set off, running across the scrubland that ran beside the dirt track.

Ketty turned to me, her whole face lit up. 'Hey, Nico, you *have* to try flying. It's the *best* thing.'

'Really?' My voice was like ice.

Ketty's face fell.

The driver revved up the Bentley. I turned away. I could still see the others reflected in the darkened windscreen in front of me.

71

There was an awkward silence for a moment, then Dylan cleared her throat.

'What about you, Hypno Boy?' she said to Ed. 'Don't you want to fly?'

'No way,' Ed said fervently. 'I got travel-sick just *looking* at you, Ketty.'

The three of them laughed. I slumped down in the passenger seat and closed my eyes.

Ten minutes later the Bentley slowed as we crunched over a gravel drive. Past a long row of what Ed informed us were eucalyptus trees, we turned a corner to see the ranch in all its glory. It was built on two levels, a large, white-washed farmhouse-style building with an array of fields behind. Its desolate situation reminded me slightly of the training camp in the Spanish desert that we'd been sent to a few weeks ago. But in all other respects, this was a building in a different league – gleaming white walls, polished wood furniture on the porch and a huge swimming pool round the side.

Cal was still miles away across the scrubland – a tiny figure jogging towards the house. As I turned to see if Ketty had noticed him, my eye was caught by a man emerging onto the porch. He was completely bald and dressed from head to toe in white – cotton trousers and a loose shirt.

'Is that Avery Jones?' Dylan asked.

Our driver nodded. He stopped the car and opened the back passenger door so Ketty and Dylan could scramble out. I got out myself, my eyes on Jones. Was it my imagination or was he staring at me?

He beckoned us over.

'Let's go,' I said.

The four of us started walking to the house. I could feel Ketty moving closer beside me, her hand reaching for mine. But I didn't take it – or even look at her. Rage was still boiling inside me.

Ketty shrank away. We walked on.

I hadn't anticipated any of this. I'd expected danger and a struggle to find Avery Jones – not a smooth, chauffeured ride straight to his luxury home.

Most of all, I hadn't expected that my main emotion as I walked up to meet him would be furious jealousy.

We reached the porch and climbed the steps. Now we were close up I could see that the man in front of us was middle-aged. At least there were lines round his eyes and mouth, though his forehead was completely smooth.

He reached forward, his smile revealing a set of perfectly white, even teeth.

'Hey there,' he said in a relaxed Australian drawl just like Cal's. He offered me his hand. 'G'day, Nico. I can't tell you how much I've looked forward to this moment.'

8: Avery Jones

Avery Jones led us into the ranch house. Even knowing nothing about interior design I could see that everything was hugely expensive. Simple leather couches, bare floors scattered with a few silk rugs and highly polished wood furniture. A huge golden statue of an elephant stood in one corner of the large, open-plan living area. Two framed abstract paintings – one of red stripes, one of blue – hung on the far wall. I was pretty sure they weren't prints.

Jones waved his hand, indicating we should sit down. 'We call this the Snug,' he said. 'Please sit down. I've asked Philly for some lemonade and snacks. Then there'll be a chance to rest and get cleaned up.'

I glanced at the others, suddenly realising how tired and grimy we all looked. It wasn't just the long journey from Helsinki – life had been fairly relentless since we'd left our hideout in the Lake District. That felt like weeks ago, though it was only a few days. Still, I wasn't ready to relax just yet.

'I think we'd like some answers before we start "chilling" with you like we're old mates,' I said. 'For a start, how did you know we were looking for you?'

'Because *I* was looking for *you*,' Avery drawled.

This wasn't the answer I expected. My heart skipped a beat.

Avery Jones smiled. 'I'd heard rumours that Geri had brought the four of you together and I knew it was true when I heard about the Wardingham explosion and Bookman's death – that was way too much of a coincidence . . . The two things *had* to be connected and *had* to be about Medusa. Wardingham was where the Medusa Project data was stored. Bookman was in charge of the whole project. Once I'd intercepted the MoD data streams and found out you were being accused of both the explosion and the murder, it was obvious to me what had happened. If Geri had turned on you, then you must have found out her big secret – that she murdered William Fox. Which means you're in real danger right now and I want to help.'

I stared at him. The way he presented the information made it sound like the most logical thing in the world, and yet how had he known any of those things for sure?

'How did you manage to read Laura's emails to Sam Hastings about coming to the airport?' Dylan said, frowning.

'When I heard about the explosion, I put an intercept on

the emails of everyone I knew connected with the Medusa Project,' Avery explained. 'Some – like Geri's personal email – were impossible to access, but Laura's was quite easy. When she emailed Sam Hastings, I was able to block the email and reply as from Hastings. She fell for it completely.'

I looked at the others. Ed and Ketty had both paled with anxiety. Dylan was still frowning.

'So you *tricked* us?' she said. 'You're admitting we've walked into a trap?'

'What about the boy who *did* meet us?' Ed said. 'Cal. How does he fit in?'

'I'll explain about Cal in a minute, but first . . .' Avery sighed. 'Look, I'm sorry for getting you here under false pretences . . . but a lie was the only way to keep you safe. Anyway, I wasn't sure you'd trust me until you'd met me in person.'

I opened my mouth to ask Avery the huge and obvious question – *why* was he doing all this? But before I could speak, Dylan was off again.

'How can we trust you?' she said angrily. 'You bought the Medusa gene code from Geri Paterson *even though* you knew she killed my dad.'

Avery studied her for a second, then sighed. 'I didn't know Geri had murdered William at the time. And I certainly didn't buy the Medusa gene code from her.'

A new tension filled the atmosphere.

'But we found the stuff you wrote about it,' I said.

'Yes, there's an article in which you *name* Medusa and hint it will soon be in your possession,' Ed added.

Avery waved his hand dismissively. 'I wrote various articles at the time arguing that William Fox was playing God with his work on genetics. However, I didn't know about Medusa back then. I went back to that blog you're referring to two days ago and *added* references to the Medusa gene so that you'd be able to find me.'

'Why?' I said, unable to hold back any longer. 'Why on earth would you go to so much trouble to help us?'

Behind me the door opened. Two blonde women – one middle-aged, the other in her twenties – walked in. Each one carried a tray loaded with drinks and sandwiches. They smiled as they set the trays down in front of Avery.

'Thank you.' He turned to us. 'These ladies are my wife, Philly, and our maid, Caro.'

'Hi,' Ed said politely.

The girls smiled. Man, how weird was this? We were all acting like we'd gone round to somebody's house and were meeting their parents.

'Two more jailers?' I said.

Avery frowned. 'You're not prisoners here, Nico. You're free to leave whenever you like. But I know you have more questions and I'm happy to answer them.' He paused. 'Now, please won't you sit and eat? We can carry on talking, but you all look half-dead from exhaustion.'

'Er . . . would you let me mind-read you first?' Ed asked.

I nodded. That was a good idea. Ed would be able to see whatever was truly inside Avery's mind.

Avery's grey eyes widened with delight. For a second, I saw a strong resemblance to Cal. Was it possible he was Cal's father?

'It would be my very great pleasure to have you mind-read me, Edward.' Avery sat forward in his sofa. 'Go ahead.'

Ed perched awkwardly next to Avery and looked into his eyes. Silence fell on the room. I eyed the platter of sandwiches. It looked tempting and I was starving. Dylan edged closer to the lemonade.

'Find out if the drink's poisoned, Ed,' she ordered.

The door to the porch slammed back on itself. I jumped. Spun round. Cal was in the doorway, thankfully now wearing his T-shirt and panting after his run.

His white-blond hair fell over his face as he grinned at Ketty.

'Hey, Ketts,' he said. 'I'm gonna take a shower. Catch you later.' He disappeared through another door.

Ketts?

I moved closer to Ketty, my irritation rising. Across the room Dylan was examining the gigantic elephant. Avery and Ed were entirely focused on each other.

'Why is he calling you Ketts?' I hissed. 'That's what *I* call you.'

Ketty looked up at me, a confused frown creasing her forehead.

'I don't know,' she whispered. 'He abbreviates lots of words. I didn't *tell* him to call me that, he just did.'

'Yeah, I noticed the two of you were getting all *bessie* mates up there in outer space.'

Ketty's frown deepened. 'Is that why you're in this horrible mood? Because you're jealous of me and *Cal*?'

'Course I'm not jealous.' I glanced over at Dylan. She was studiously ignoring us, peering at an elegant gold ornament on the sideboard across the room. 'I just thought it was a bit odd that—'

'Well, what did you see, Ed?' Avery asked.

I looked around. Avery was sitting back in the sofa, arms folded, an amused expression on his face.

Ed turned to me and Ketty. 'Everything Avery's told us is true. He wants to help us because he knows about the Medusa gene killing our mothers and he knows how powerful and dangerous Geri is.'

Dylan walked towards us. 'What about the lemonade?'

'It's fine – and, apparently, delicious,' Ed said.

'Good.' Dylan poured herself a huge glass.

Avery sat forward and poured four more. I looked at Ketty. She had tucked her hair behind her ears and had gone to sit on a sofa across the room from me, her mouth set in a grim line.

I sank into the nearest seat and accepted the glass of lemonade Avery offered me. He was right – it was delicious. But I barely tasted it and, suddenly, I wasn't really hungry for sandwiches any more either.

Everything was usually so easy with Ketty – what was going wrong?

Why couldn't she see that her rushing off with Cal without saying anything was bound to make me feel annoyed? And it wasn't just Cal . . . it was this whole set-up. Maybe Avery Jones *did* want to help us, but he'd still tricked us into coming here.

Dylan and Ed munched on hunks of bread. Ketty nibbled at a carrot stick. Without warning, Ed appeared in my head.

You okay, Nico?

I'm great, thanks, I thought-spoke, knowing Ed would be able to see I was absolutely not great.

I just wanted to say it's true, Avery seems on the level. There's just one thing . . . .

What?

D'you remember that guy, Foster, from a few months back . . . the one I had to mind-read so we could find out where he was holding Ketty's brother hostage?

Yes. I remembered it well. Ed had actually vomited after that mind-reading session, claiming that Foster had 'held' his mind in a way Ed had never experienced before.

Well, I got the sense that Avery could do what Foster did to me back then. He just chose not to. Ed hesitated. *It's hard to explain, but he has a very ordered mind. It's not chaotic like most people's and . . . I can't be sure because*

*he's so controlled, but I think there might be stuff he's
hiding . . . er, like . . . er . . . behind mental walls.*

Okay, thanks for the warning.

Ed broke the connection and I looked up – to find
Avery staring at me. He looked away immediately, a
strange expression on his face. He fixed his gaze on the
lemonade glass I'd been drinking from, seemingly lost
in thought.

A shiver snaked down my back. Whatever anyone said,
I wasn't going to trust Avery Jones without a lot more proof
that he truly had our best interests at heart.

Avery shook himself and looked up.

'I hope, now that Ed has used his amazing gift to see
inside my mind, that you will begin to trust me. I only want
to help you. I'm offering you the chance to stay here –
where Geri Paterson will never find you – while you work
out what to do next. I have plenty of money and there's
plenty of space. I ask only that you let me talk to you about
your gifts. As a psychologist, I was always convinced that
the Medusa gene would work differently in different
people. The four of you, with your varying abilities, seem
to prove me right.'

'Can we call our parents?' Ketty asked. 'I mean, without
the phone calls being traced?'

'Of course,' Avery said. 'I'll sort out some safe phones
to be secretly delivered to your parents. You can use the
secure line here to call them.'

'Wait a minute,' Dylan said. 'If Geri didn't sell you the

81

Medusa gene, how d'you explain Cal? Why is he here? How come he's able to fly, for Pete's sake?'

'Ah, yes . . . Cal . . .' Avery hesitated. 'I wanted to give you some background first, but . . . well . . . yes, I have a child with the Medusa gene.'

'Cal is your *son*?' Ketty said. She was open-mouthed, clearly completely fascinated.

'I thought so,' I said, trying to sound knowing. The others looked at me.

'Yeah, we forgot.' Dylan rolled her eyes. 'You know everything, Nico.'

'Yes, Cal is my son,' Avery said lightly. 'And, before you ask, he's the only one with the Medusa gene. I'll tell you the full story later . . . For now I hope you will let me show you to your rooms. Everyone has their own en suite and—'

'Excuse me for butting into the invite to the freakin' spa weekend,' Dylan said, looking around at everybody. 'But we can't *stay*. We came here to get evidence against Geri, remember? So we can clear our names of Bookman's murder and get her sent to jail for what she did to my parents.' She turned on Avery. 'You don't have any proof that she killed my dad, do you?'

'No,' Avery said. 'I don't.'

There was a short pause.

'We can stay for a bit,' Ketty said, her tone calm and reasonable. 'Don't you think, Ed?'

Why was she asking him? It struck me that she hadn't

so much as looked in my direction since our earlier argument.

Ed glanced nervously at Dylan. 'It makes sense to stay for a day or two,' he said. 'I mean, I'm certain Professor Jones doesn't want to hurt us. And we're going to need some time to work out what to do next so that we can prove Geri's a murderer and get back home, so . . .'

'You're all missing the point,' I said, standing up. Ed's words about Avery's powerful, hidden thoughts suddenly made sense. 'Avery might not want to hurt us, but he's definitely planning on using us.'

Avery gazed up at me, eyebrows raised. There was a steely quality in his expression, but when he spoke, his voice was smooth and good-humoured.

'And how am I planning on using you, Nico?' he said.

'I don't know yet,' I said. 'But I don't believe you went to all the trouble of bringing us here just out of the goodness of your heart.'

The tension in the room rose. I could feel the others looking intently at me, but I kept my gaze on Avery.

He gave a low chuckle. 'You're quite right, Nico. I didn't bring you here just as an act of charity. I thought this could wait a day or two, but evidently it needs to come out now.' He paused. 'There *is* something I want – but it's something you want, too. In fact, it's something you need.'

The room was now so silent I could hear the low hum of the air conditioner.

'And what's that?' I said.

Avery looked at Dylan. 'I told you just now that I had no concrete evidence that Geri killed your parents?'

Dylan nodded. Avery's hard, grey eyes flickered from her across the others, coming to rest on me.

'Well, that was true,' he said. 'I don't have any proof. But I know where you can get it.'

9: Thefts

Avery refused to tell us any more about the evidence on Geri until we had showered and rested. He took us through a series of cool, shady corridors and up a small flight of stairs to what he referred to as the east wing of the house. With a wave of his hand, he indicated four rooms, two on either side of a long landing that led to a balcony overlooking the swimming pool.

The rooms were identical. Spacious and minimalist, with soft brown covers and cushions on the beds and glass-topped bedside tables. Each room had a small wardrobe with hanging space and drawers and an en suite bathroom. A huge, flat-screen TV stood in the corner, complete with a cupboard full of computer games and DVDs.

'You can use the internet in here . . . download movies . . . music . . . whatever you like . . .' Avery said, smiling at our amazement.

'It's like a freakin' hotel,' said Dylan.

'Yes, and you are my guests,' Avery said smoothly. 'So

please ask for anything you need.' He checked his watch – large and gold and the only piece of jewellery he wore.

'I realise you must be disoriented because of the time difference with England, but it's now almost six p.m. Why don't you relax for an hour, then I'll send Cal to take you on a tour of the ranch? After that, I'll join you for dinner.'

'Thank you,' said Ed politely. Ketty and Dylan nodded.

I leaned against the wall of the bedroom we were standing in. Was I the only one who felt that something was massively off here? It just all felt too good to be true.

I looked up. Avery was staring at me again. His eyes flickered away immediately and he cleared his throat.

'If you'd like to take a shower, there are towels in the bathrooms,' he said. 'I'll send Philly with a change of clothes.'

'What, you just happen to have a load of clothes that'll fit us in the house?' I said suspiciously.

Avery smiled. 'I can't promise the fit will be exact, or that the garments will be to your taste, but I have eight children, ranging in age from three to twenty-three – so, yes, there're plenty of clothes in the house!'

'Eight children?' Ketty said faintly.

'And you said *none* of them apart from Cal are Medusa?' Dylan asked.

'That's right,' said Avery.

'Are they all here?' Ed asked.

'No.' Avery explained. 'The three eldest are away at college or work. The others are here. You'll see them later

– the younger ones are mine and Philly's children. The older ones belong to my late first and second wives.'

'Three wives and eight children?' I glared at Avery. 'Are you trying to set some kind of record?'

Avery's gaze hardened for a second, then he pursed his lips. 'As I said, both my first and second wives died. It is to Philly's great credit that she treats all my children as her own,' he said, an edge creeping into his voice. 'Please don't judge the way I live my life, Nico. We do the best we can.'

He took his leave and disappeared along the corridor. As soon as he'd gone, the others rounded on me.

'Why were you so rude?' Ketty demanded.

'Yeah,' Dylan agreed. 'The guy's a weirdo, for sure, but we don't want to get him mad until we've found out about the evidence he's got on Geri.'

I stomped across the bedroom to the window. This room looked out over a patch of grass surrounded by rose bushes. I couldn't imagine the effort it must take in this dust bowl to keep anything green alive. I could just make out the edge of the swimming pool outside. The water shimmered in the sunlight.

It was all too perfect . . . too beautiful . . .

'I don't believe he knows anything about any evidence against Geri,' I snarled. 'I think he's making it up. Did you see the way he keeps looking at me? Like I'm a bug under a microscope.'

Ketty rolled her eyes. 'You are such an egotist, Nico. You're imagining the looks – and I think you're being paranoid about Avery. Why shouldn't he want to help us expose Geri?'

'What's in it for him?' I demanded.

'Maybe he wants revenge, too,' Dylan said. 'If Cal's his son, then he must have had a relationship with Cal's mother – who must have been killed by the Medusa gene, like our moms were.'

'She'd be one of his late wives.' Ketty nodded. 'What do you think, Ed?'

'Er . . . I don't think Avery was lying about either the evidence on Geri or about looking after us here for a while,' Ed said slowly. 'Though I agree with Nico that there's something he's not telling us.'

'Well, I'm taking a shower,' Dylan said. 'We can find out everything else later.'

She marched into the room opposite and shut the door. Ed wandered away soon after, to the room immediately beyond Dylan's. Ketty turned to go.

I grabbed her arm. 'Ketts?' I said. 'What's up?'

She shook off my arm. 'Nothing.'

'Yes, there is,' I said. 'Why are you mad at me?'

'Why are you being so difficult?' she said.

I stared at her. Did she really think *I* was the one being difficult?

'Why's it unreasonable to be suspicious of a man who comes out of nowhere and offers us exactly what we want, plus the equivalent of a holiday in a five-star hotel?'

'I'm not talking about Avery,' Ketty said. 'I'm talking

about Cal. Why did you make all that fuss about him taking me flying earlier?'

'I *didn't* make a fuss,' I insisted. 'I just thought you could have talked to me – and the others – before you went off with Cal.'

Ketty shook her head. 'Like you talked to us before you went off with Amy back to England?'

What?

'That's completely different,' I said. 'Taking you with me would have put you in danger.'

'But you didn't even discuss it,' Ketty said. 'You just went off on your own, like you always do. And for far longer.'

I opened my mouth to protest, but Ketty held up her hand. 'Don't, Nico.' She paused. 'Just think about it. I'm going to my room.'

She turned on her heel and disappeared inside the room next door. I stood, staring after her. Was she right? Was me going off with Amy back to England a similar thing to her going off with Cal to try out his Medusa gift? It was true that I hadn't said anything, but that was because I knew there'd just have been an argument. And at least I was trying to help the four of us get evidence on Geri. Ketty had just been messing around with Cal.

And he'd *definitely* been flirting with her.

I gritted my teeth and went back inside my room. I took a long, hot bath in the massive bathtub, then wrapped myself in a white, fluffy towel. None of this improved my mood.

As I paced back into the bedroom, there was a knock on the door. Avery's wife, Philly, was outside, four carrier bags in her hands.

She looked at me with soft eyes. 'Nico?'

I nodded, checking my towel was firmly wrapped round me.

She handed me one of the bags. 'Something in there should fit.'

'How long have you lived here?' I said, too curious to keep silent.

'Avery and I moved here just after our youngest was born.' She paused.

'What about Cal?' I said. 'What happened to his mum?'

'Meg?' Philly lowered her voice. 'She died, of course. But you know about that. Your mother died for the same reason, didn't she?'

I nodded again. Philly smiled sympathetically at me. 'Avery will answer all your questions,' she said. 'Get dressed. Cal will be along to collect you in fifteen minutes.'

She drifted along the corridor to Ketty's door. I closed mine and examined the contents of my bag. Two pairs of plain grey shorts which fitted fine and a selection of T-shirts. I picked one in a pale green that I knew I'd look good in, then spent a bit of time sorting my hair.

Don't get me wrong – I'm not vain or anything, but I like making the most of how I look. So many guys either don't know how or can't be bothered. I mean, look at Ed!

I examined my torso in the bathroom mirror before

slipping on my T-shirt. I looked okay, though my muscles weren't anywhere near as developed as Cal's. And though my arms were a deeper brown than his, the rest of my torso was much paler, where it had been hidden from the sun for months.

I made a mental note that whatever else I did in the next couple of days, I was going to make an effort to build myself up a bit. Avery was bound to have a gym here. And I was definitely going to get outside in the sunshine.

Another knock on the door. This time Cal was outside. He looked at me without smiling. 'The others are ready. You?' His tone was curt.

It struck me that he'd been ruder to me than the others right from the start. Or at least, right from the moment he'd clocked Ketty.

I narrowed my eyes. 'I'm ready,' I said.

Cal stared at me. *Man*, he looked mad as hell. I met his gaze. No way was this jerk intimidating me.

The others emerged from their rooms. Dylan was dressed in a flowery, feminine dress rather like the one Caro, the maid, had worn earlier. Ketty was in cut-off jeans and a pretty T-shirt. Ed – unbelievably – was wearing crisp cotton trousers and a polo shirt, – almost an exact copy of his normal dress style back home.

'Hey, Chino Boy,' Dylan said, ruffling his hair. 'How you doing?'

Ed grunted.

Cal's eyes lingered on Ketty. I gave him a not particularly gentle prod in the ribs. 'Shall we go?' I said.

Cal led us along the landing to the balcony at the end. It was set with plants and sunloungers and overlooked the swimming pool below and the small garden area beyond.

As we followed Cal down the steps to the swimming pool patio, I gazed out across the scrubland beyond. There was literally nothing for miles, just the mountains in one direction and the outline of the nearest town in the other.

'This is the pool area,' Cal said.

'*Really?*' I said.

Ketty glared at me. Dylan giggled.

Ignoring my interruption, Cal led us round the corner to the back of the ranch. Fenced fields stretched out as far as the eye could see. Cal started droning on about how many zillions of hectares belonged to the ranch. Apparently, there were sheep out there somewhere – towards the greener part of the landscape.

Two horses gambolled in one of the nearer fields.

'Can we ride them?' Dylan asked breathlessly.

'Sure,' said Cal.

Dylan's eyes glittered. 'You have to try riding, Ketty. It's awesome. As good as flying, I imagine.'

'D'you wanna go flying with me now?' Cal said with what looked to me like a very self-satisfied smirk on his face.

'*Sooo* much,' said Dylan.

'What about you?' Cal turned to Ketty. 'You want to come up again, too?'

I glared at her. Surely she wasn't going to fall for his fake charm *again*.

'I'd love to,' she said.

I ground my teeth. Couldn't she see he was totally hitting on her?

Cal grinned. 'Okay, let me show Dylan how it works first.'

He grabbed her wrist and they soared into the air.

Ed clutched his chest. 'There is no way I'm ever doing that,' he said.

Cal did a quick spin over the ranch with Dylan. She squealed with delight. I glanced at Ketty. She was watching – enraptured.

After a few minutes Cal and Dylan landed beside us.

'That was *sooo* awesome,' Dylan said. 'Let's go again.'

'I can take you both up, if you like.' Cal spoke to Ketty, completely ignoring me and Ed. 'It'll be totally safe.'

'Really?' Ketty's eyes shone as he took her hand.

As the three of them soared into the air, I clenched my fists. If I hadn't been sure before, I was now. Cal was definitely trying to steal my girlfriend – and from right under my nose.

At that moment, Avery came out of the house and strolled towards us. He stood between me and Ed, smoothing his bald head with his hand.

'Do you have everything you need?' he asked us politely.

Yeah, except for a way of getting rid of Cal or any idea what you're really after.

I said nothing.

'Yes, thank you,' Ed replied.

I could feel Avery's eyes on me again. I turned to face him.

'What?' I said, knowing I sounded rude and not caring.

Avery looked at me thoughtfully. 'I know you're impatient for answers, Nico, and I *have* answers. The evidence that will convict Geri Paterson of murder and help prove your innocence is her own confession.'

I blinked at him, startled by his sudden reference back to our main reason for being here. Ed's mouth fell open.

'Go on,' I said.

'Geri sold the Medusa gene code to a Scottish scientist called Rod McMurdo,' Avery said. 'She met him during her early days as a psychic investigator. In fact, it was McMurdo who told her about William Fox. Fox and McMurdo didn't know each other, but Fox was a big name in scientific circles. McMurdo had some interesting ideas, but he wasn't in William Fox's league as a scientist. When Geri discovered Fox, she lost interest in McMurdo who left the UK to work here in Sydney. Later, after Fox's death, Geri flew over to sell McMurdo the gene code and he recorded her explaining exactly how far she'd gone to bring it to him.'

'She just blurted out that she'd murdered someone?' I said, disbelieving.

'She was in an emotional state,' Avery said. 'And to be honest, I think she *wanted* to confess to someone. She knew that as long as McMurdo had possession of the gene, which he desperately wanted, he would never expose her.'

'And how do you know all this?' I demanded.

'McMurdo and I used to be friends. We met here in Sydney . . . we worked at the same hospital for a while. McMurdo knew that I'd had a number of run-ins with William Fox . . . we even chatted about how ludicrous Fox's claims were. At the time, neither of us believed that the Medusa gene really existed.' Avery sighed. 'Anyway, when my second wife, Meg, became pregnant, McMurdo told us he had bought the Medusa gene.'

'Did he tell you about the mothers dying?' I asked.

'No, not that,' Avery said. 'McMurdo must have known that the Medusa gene was deadly – after all, Geri had sold him the gene – but he certainly didn't tell us. The implantation worked. Cal was born and . . .'

'. . . and a few years later Cal's mother – Meg – died,' Ed said.

Avery nodded, looking weary.

'So you want revenge on McMurdo?' I said slowly.

'Yes, he betrayed me, just as Geri betrayed you,' Avery said bitterly. 'I went after him at the time, but he was clever . . . there was no proof he'd ever been involved in Cal's birth.'

'Why didn't you just beat him up?' I said.

Avery stared at me. 'Physical violence is not my style,

95

Nico.' He sighed. 'I've waited a long time for this, but if you can find the proof that Geri killed William Fox, McMurdo goes down with her as an accessory after the fact. It's not the crime I wanted him to pay for most, but it will have to do.'

I nodded. It made sense.

Avery cleared his throat. 'I hope you'll understand, Nico, but before I tell you any more, I'd like to see what you're capable of. McMurdo is potentially a dangerous man and I need to know you can take care of yourself.'

My immediate reaction was resentment. What did he think I was – some sort of performing chimp? But I soon realised it was in my interests to show Avery exactly what I could do. If we could access McMurdo's secret film of Geri's confession, then we could hand it over to the Australian police. It was perfect, in fact. Geri might have a lot of power at home in Britain, but even she couldn't control a police force on the other side of the world.

'Sure, I'll show you what I can do.' I looked around for something to move telekinetically that would impress Avery. Apart from a couple of bales of hay in the neighbouring field and the sunloungers round the pool behind us, there wasn't much that was movable out here. And I was certain Avery wouldn't want me ripping up his plants or fences.

My gaze flickered upwards, to where Cal, with Ketty and Dylan on either side, were lined up in the air about twenty metres above the ground, performing double somersaults.

Without thinking it through, I focused all my powers on the three of them. I only intended to give them a nudge, to throw their stupid somersaults off balance, but the energy flowed out of me with more force than I'd realised.

The three of them blasted forwards in the air, as if shoved by an invisible hand. With a yell, Cal let go of both girls' hands.

And then everything went into slow motion as the three of them dropped through the air, falling towards the ground.

10: Falling

I could feel myself trying to race forwards, but everything had slowed and it was like moving through mud. Beside me, Avery roared out Cal's name.

I held out my shaking hands. Dylan and Ketty were dropping like stones. I put every ounce of effort I had into the telekinesis, intending to hold them up.

And then I realised Cal had the girls by the arms again. They bobbed in the air for a moment, then soared up.

They were safe. The whole thing had lasted seconds.

My heart thudded as it occurred to me that Dylan – had she fallen – would have been safe thanks to her ability to protect herself from physical harm. Ketty, on the other hand, would probably have fallen to her death if Cal or I hadn't saved her.

Avery and Ed were still standing beside me, looking shocked. Above our heads, Cal and Dylan were speaking. Cal let go of Dylan's arm and she dropped to earth.

Avery gasped, but it was obvious from the relaxed

way Dylan fell that she was fine. She landed lightly on the ground, her force field protecting her from the impact. Jumping up, she raced towards us, her eyes glinting with fury.

'Good job, Nico,' she said venomously. 'I'm here to tell you you're a total freakin' jerk.'

I froze. Avery was looking at me now, his eyes still wide with shock.

Ed frowned. 'Dylan's right,' he said angrily. 'What were you thinking? If Cal hadn't caught Ketty, she'd have really hurt herself.'

'I'd have brought her down okay,' I said. But inside my stomach was twisting over. Ketty had been totally vulnerable up there.

My face grew hot as I thought of how terrified she must have been. I looked up, desperate for her to come back so I could apologise, but she and Cal were now just distant specks in the sky.

It was dark and Cal and Ketty still weren't back and I was quietly going off my head.

Ed had contacted Ketty remotely, so I knew she was safe – but when I borrowed his phone to call her, it went straight to voicemail, so I still hadn't had a chance to apologise.

We were in the dining room, sitting round a huge oak table with Avery, Philly and Caro – and the four little kids Avery had mentioned earlier. They were all under ten and with the same white-blond hair as Cal. Shy at first, they were soon chatting happily with Ed and Dylan. I didn't talk much myself. I was too busy wondering where Cal and Ketty were – and what they were doing.

Avery sat me next to him at the head of the table. He'd already informed me we'd be eating shepherd's pie – 'an English dish for our English visitors' – but had made no mention of my disastrous telekinesis demonstration outside.

As Philly put a steaming portion of mince and potato in front of me, Ketty and Cal appeared in the doorway. They were laughing, leaning against each other and Ketty's hair was all tousled. I stared at her, feeling my face flush. Couldn't she see how humiliating it was for her to be so friendly with him?

'You're late,' Avery barked.

The atmosphere tensed. The two women looked at each other and even the smallest child shrank back in his seat. I got the distinct impression that, for all his easy, relaxed manner, Avery in a temper was not a pretty sight.

Cal straightened up immediately. 'Sorry, sir,' he said. *Sir*. I grinned.

Ketty blushed bright red. She scurried to the nearest seat, next to Dylan. Cal went round the other side of the table and slid in between two of the younger kids.

Seconds later Philly had served them both and everyone was laughing and chatting again.

Everyone except me. I kept looking over, trying to catch

Ketty's eye, but she was intent on her conversation with Dylan and avoided my gaze. Cal kept looking over at her, too. He glanced once at my end of the table, scowled and looked resolutely away again.

I gritted my teeth. That was it. The sooner we left here the better. I turned to Avery. Once again, he was already watching me. I shook off the slightly spooked feeling this gave me.

'I'd like to get hold of this film showing Geri Paterson's confession as soon as possible,' I said. 'Where do you think McMurdo keeps it?'

'I don't know,' Avery said. 'But it should be easy enough to find McMurdo himself. Apart from the hospital where he still does some consultancy work, he's on the board of a number of organisations in Sydney.'

'Where's he going to be tomorrow?'

Avery looked startled. '*Tomorrow?*'

'There's no point hanging around,' I said.

Avery chuckled. 'I'll get one of my men to call his secretary . . . pretend to be a client . . . It won't be hard to find out . . .'

A few minutes later we had our answer. Tomorrow morning McMurdo was going to be attending a board meeting at a small art gallery in Sydney of which he was patron.

'Good,' I said, thinking it through. Dylan, Ketty and I could create a diversion while Ed mind-read McMurdo to find out where the film of Geri's confession was hidden.

A thought suddenly struck me. 'How do you know McMurdo hasn't destroyed the evidence by now?'

'I don't,' Avery said. 'But I doubt it. It's his insurance against Geri and McMurdo once told me he'd left instructions for the confession to be sent to the police if anything happened to him.'

Half an hour later the meal finished and Avery suggested we go and sit outside, by the pool, to talk through the details of the plan. Everyone agreed, but instead of heading straight outside onto the terrace, I made my way round the table to Ketty.

'Ketts,' I said firmly. 'Can I have a word?'

She looked up and there was real sadness in her eyes. 'Hi.'

I took a deep breath. 'I'm really sorry I was such a jerk earlier. It was stupid of me to use telekinesis when you were up in the air and I didn't mean to push you so that you fell.'

Ketty nodded. Around us the room was still bustling, but no one was paying us particular attention. Avery was talking in a low voice to Ed as they headed outside, while Philly and Caro dealt with the smaller kids. Dylan had stopped Cal on his way round the table and they were now deep in conversation, too.

'Ketts?' I said. 'Are we okay?'

She looked up at me again. 'Sure,' she said, forcing a smile.

I smiled back, but somewhere inside I still felt uneasy.

Despite Ketty's smile, she looked sad. But I didn't know what else to say and there was no time for a longer conversation.

A few minutes later Ketty, Ed, Dylan, Avery, Cal and I were sitting at one of the wrought-iron tables between the pool and the rose garden. As we talked, both Dylan and Ed made some useful suggestions. Avery sat back in his chair, watching us thoughtfully. Ketty and Cal said nothing until I'd finished, then Ketty bit her lip.

'I get what each of us is supposed to do,' she said, 'and it makes sense. But what about Cal? He'd be really useful for helping Ed and Dylan get away.'

'This thing with Geri hasn't got anything to do with Cal,' I said quickly. He was the last person I wanted involved.

'Yes, it does.' Cal glared at me. 'She knew the Medusa gene would kill all the mums and she still sold it to McMurdo. As far as I'm concerned, she killed my mother – that gives me as good a reason to want Geri behind bars as the rest of you.'

Dylan and Ed nodded. I kept my eyes on Ketty. She was gazing at Cal with . . . was that admiration?

'Okay,' I said uncertainly. 'But the four of us are used to working together. It won't be easy to adapt to someone else being on the team.'

Dylan snorted. 'I think we'll cope,' she said, her voice dripping with irritation.

'It'll work better with Cal,' Ed said.

I met Ketty's eyes. It was obvious that she, like the others, really wanted Cal to join us – and she'd just see any further objections I made as me being difficult again. I knew I had to give in – and with good grace, too.

'Sure.' I attempted what I hoped was a charming smile. 'Welcome to the Medusa Project, Cal.'

He nodded curtly.

It wasn't late, but we were all yawning, our body clocks totally thrown by the time difference with the UK. Avery gently shooed us back to our rooms, with the promise that we could set off for McMurdo's art gallery in the morning.

I was hoping for a bit of private time with Ketty, but she disappeared into her room before I had the chance. In the end I slept worse than I'd ever slept in my life – waking every few hours, all disoriented, my head full of images of Cal and Ketty together.

The morning was hot and sticky. Everybody seemed on edge.

'Are you sure you wouldn't rather rest today and go after McMurdo tomorrow?' Avery asked.

'No,' I said before anyone else had a chance to speak. 'We need to get on with this.'

Avery himself drove the five of us into town. He had a jeep – not as cool as the Bentley, but with room for all of us in the back. That suited me. The last thing I wanted was Cal offering to fly Ketty all the way to Sydney.

It took over an hour to drive to the outskirts of Sydney and nearly another fifty minutes to reach McMurdo's art gallery. Avery dropped us at the end of the road.

'Remember, you mustn't let anyone see what you're capable of,' he warned Cal. 'If you have to fly, do it discreetly, and stop as soon as you're out of immediate danger.'

'Yes, sir,' Cal said. He looked around sulkily, as if wondering why his dad wasn't lecturing the rest of us.

'We'll look after Cal,' I said, knowing this would annoy him.

'I know you will.' Avery smiled at me. 'Okay, Cal, remember Nico's in charge. You do what he says.'

'Yes, sir,' Cal said again.

I grinned. As we walked towards the art gallery, I put my arm round Ketty's shoulders. To my relief, she didn't shrug me off.

'How's it going with the visions? Seen anything we should know about?' I asked with a smile.

Ketty shook her head. 'I got a few glimpses earlier – just the inside of the gallery with the atrium where we're going to stand – but it's gone again now. It *always* gets flaky when I'm stressed.'

'I know, babe,' I said. 'But it'll come back – I've got faith.'

Ketty smiled at me. My spirits soared. Everything was looking up: Ketty wasn't mad any more, Avery had put Cal in his place – and I was in charge of this mission.

The other four stared at me expectantly as we entered the art gallery. We were all wearing caps pulled low over our foreheads, except Cal who was in a supersize hoodie. None of the cameras could possibly pick up our faces.

I checked the watch Avery had lent me. 'It's 11.03,' I said quietly. 'Ketty and I will distract the guards in two minutes. You guys ready?'

Ed and Dylan nodded. Cal offered me a scowl.

'Let's go.' Keeping my head down, I took Ketty's hand again and we wandered into the main room of the gallery. As Avery had described the night before – and Ketty had just prefigured – it was an atrium, with a high glass roof two floors above our heads. Stairs led up to a balcony that overlooked the ground floor where we were standing.

The room was bright with sunshine and full of people – several twenty- and thirty-somethings wandering around in pairs, plus a school party at the far end. I checked the time again as we wandered past the colourful paintings that covered all the walls. Ketty tucked a few stray hairs under her cap, and pulled the shapeless grey sweat top she was wearing closer round her.

My heart beat fast as I surveyed the room, looking for a suitable picture. Nothing too large or cumbersome.

My eyes lit on a small painting in the corner – abstract blue stripes against a russet-coloured background. It was conveniently positioned above a radiator. I glanced around again. No one was directly watching either the picture or me.

Making as small a movement with my hands as I could, I twisted my right wrist. The picture jumped off the wall. I lowered it carefully – but very quickly – behind the radiator below. As I did so, an alarm sounded.

Everyone in the room looked up. A security guard on the ground floor spun round, quickly spotting the missing picture.

'It's been taken!' he yelled. 'Look.' He pointed at the gap in the wall where the painting had hung.

The atrium erupted with yells. I looked down, hiding the smile that was spreading across my face.

So far so good.

11: The Gallery

Voices rose over the alarm as two security guards came running past us. I shrank back against the wall, making sure I kept my face well out of sight.

'My turn,' Ketty whispered. She followed the two guards to the scene of the crime. People were crowding round the place on the wall where the painting had hung though so far no one had spotted it tucked deep behind the radiator. Ketty thrust herself into the crowd.

The noise was deafening, the gallery acoustics managing to magnify everyone's shouts. I could just make out Ketty's shriek above the other voices.

'There were three of them,' she yelled, pointing towards the fire exit. 'They took the painting and ran off through there.'

More shrieks and yells. I waited, adrenalin surging through me.

A few moments later and Ketty appeared at my side. 'Let's get to the meeting point,' she said.

We raced outside. Police sirens were now sounding in the distance. Ketty and I took a left, towards Avery's car which was still parked at the end of the street. He was leaning on the bonnet, waiting for us.

He leaped up as we approached, relief all over his face.

'You're okay?' he said.

'Course.' I looked back at the art gallery. A police car had just pulled up and someone was putting crime-scene tape around the area outside the front door.

'That's overkill, isn't it?' Avery murmured.

I shrugged. 'They probably haven't found the painting behind the radiator yet. Ketty threw them off the scent, but they'll see it as soon as all the fuss dies down.'

Avery chuckled.

Another police car arrived. We waited for the others to appear. After ten minutes Avery was getting agitated.

'What's happening?' he said. 'The others should be out by now.'

I peered down the road. Why hadn't Ed made contact?

Ketty gasped. 'They're coming . . . Cal and Dylan . . . they're jumping . . . flying . . . I just saw a flash of it . . . a vision . . . We should see them any second.'

As she finished speaking, the two of them raced round the corner. They were both running hard, Cal slightly in the lead. Dylan's red hair streamed out behind her. They stopped in front of us, panting.

'It's Ed.' Dylan grabbed my arm. 'Major meltdown. You've got to go back for him, Nico.'

'What happened?' Ketty said breathlessly.

'We got to the office where McMurdo was having his meeting just as the alarm went off,' Dylan said. 'Everyone rushed out. No one even noticed us.'

'What about McMurdo?' I said.

'Cal distracted his PA while Ed and I followed him back into his office,' Dylan went on.

'Then I kept watch,' Cal added, 'while Ed mind-read McMurdo to find out where the film of Geri's confession is.'

'And?' I demanded. 'What went wrong?'

'It was when we left the office,' Dylan said, twisting her hair round her hand. 'Cal was outside, waiting for us. He said police were coming up the stairs and we had to jump out of the first-storey window. I was cool with that, but Ed totally freaked. Refused to jump with Cal. I have no idea why. He jumped from much higher up from that church tower with you back in Africa.'

'So you just *left* him there?' I turned accusingly from Dylan to Cal.

Cal shrugged. He didn't look any less sulky than when we'd entered the art gallery twenty minutes ago. 'We didn't have a choice. Ed ran away. He won't be able to leave the building, not with all the security downstairs. If Dylan and I hadn't jumped, we'd be stuck there, too.'

'I'll get him,' Avery said, locking the jeep.

'No. If McMurdo sees you, it'll give everything away,' I said. 'I should go. Ed knows exactly what I can do. Maybe

110

he'll even try contacting me telepathically. I can get him out of wherever they're holding him.'

'Why would they hold him?' Ketty asked.

'They're holding everybody,' Dylan explained. 'Trying to work out what happened to their stupid painting.'

I broke into a run.

'Wait for me.' Ketty was pounding along beside me.

Seconds later we reached the art gallery.

'Where on earth is he?' I said, looking along the front of the building. A crowd had gathered now. The alarm was still sounding.

Ketty was silent. I turned to her. Her eyes were glazed over. Was she having a vision or receiving telepathic communication from Ed?

As I watched, she snapped out of it.

'Ed just made contact . . . says he panicked,' she reported. 'He's in the gallery with the other visitors, waiting to be interviewed by the police. Apparently, McMurdo's down there, too, and Ed's all freaked out in case he recognises him from the mind-reading.'

'Man . . .'

'Oh, Nico, suppose he can't handle it.' Ketty clasped her hands together. 'Suppose he blurts everything out to the security guards?'

'We won't let that happen,' I reassured her.

I thought through the plans of the art gallery we'd pored over that morning. There was a disabled toilet at the end of the corridor, to the right of the main gallery.

As I worked this through, Ed appeared in my head.

Ketty says you're outside, he thought-spoke.

I told him to get to the disabled loo – and to stay tele-pathically connected – then raced round the corner to where its window was visible from the street. People were crowding nearby, but all of them were watching the gallery entrance.

'I'm going to get him out through there,' I explained to Ketty, pointing to the window of the disabled toilet. 'Stay here and shout if anyone comes.'

Ketty nodded. I raced along to the toilet. The window was just above my head, about two metres off the floor.

Ed? I thought-spoke. *Are you there?*

I'm in the cubicle. Nico, I'm sorry, but I couldn't jump out of that window upstairs. It was Cal . . . I didn't . . . I just don't know him well enough to—

Never mind that now. Can you reach the toilet window?

Yes, but it's locked.

I looked up at the outer wall of the toilet, focusing hard on the frame above my head. I raised my hands. I couldn't see the whole of the outer part of the lock from this angle, but I'd opened locks like this a million times.

I gave my wrist a flick and heard the satisfying click of the window opening. A second later Ed's hand appeared on the sill. I focused on helping him up telekinetically, trying to move him as smoothly as I could.

He rose, his face screwed up in concentration.

Okay? I thought-spoke.

Yeah, this is weird, though.

Ed pushed at the glass, opening the window further. A moment later he was scrabbling his way through. I caught his eye and, in that moment, felt a surge of pride. Ed might not have trusted Cal, but he *was* willing to put himself in my hands as he had done before, in that jump from the church tower in Africa.

'Turn around,' I ordered.

Ed twisted round so that he faced the wall.

'Okay, now let go, I've got you,' I said, focusing on holding him in the air.

I felt my telekinesis taking his weight, as Ed stopped clinging onto the window frame. I took a quick moment to balance him, then gently teleported him to the ground.

As he landed, I glanced up to where Ketty was still keeping lookout at the end of the street.

'Go with Ketty,' I said.

Ed nodded. 'Er, thanks . . .'

'No sweat.'

Ed set off. I looked up at the toilet window again. Two flicks of my wrist and it was shut and locked. As I stepped back, about to run to the others, something made me look up.

A man with cropped, grey hair and dark brown eyes was peering out of the open first-floor window immediately above the toilets. I recognised him straight away from the photos we'd studied earlier. Rod McMurdo.

I froze.

113

As our eyes met, McMurdo's mouth fell open. '*Nico?*'

Heart pounding, I turned and ran, tugging my cap down over my face as I tore out of the alley towards Avery and the waiting car.

McMurdo hadn't lived in the UK for fifteen years.

How on earth had he known who I was?

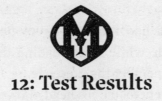

12: Test Results

I reached Avery's car just behind Ed and Ketty. Seconds later we were zooming down the road.

The others chattered away, full of that combination of excitement and relief that comes after a mission nearly goes wrong, then works out at the last minute. I sat in silence, going over what had just happened. How could I have been so careless? We'd kept our faces away from all the security staff and indoor cameras. Why hadn't I thought there might be someone watching us outside?

Ed was eager to report that he'd seen exactly where McMurdo was keeping Geri's filmed confession.

'It's in his bank, in a safety deposit box,' he said. 'I know the name and the branch, and the number of the box, though it won't be easy to access once we're inside.'

Dylan snorted. 'Don't be so lame. We'll do it.'

'Are you sure McMurdo won't remember your face from the mind-reading?' I said. It had occurred to me that maybe McMurdo knew more about *all* of us than we'd realised.

'No,' Ed said firmly. 'I did the full memory-erasing technique on him.'

I nodded. Ed had recently developed the ability to hypnotise people while mind-reading them so that they would never remember his presence.

'When you were inside his head, did you see if he knew you?' I said. 'Or if he knew the rest of us?'

'No.' Ed frowned. 'I wasn't looking for that information though, so—'

'There's no way McMurdo could know what any of you look like,' Avery said. 'Geri kept you all well hidden away. We just knew your code names . . . Cobra, Mamba, Sidewinder and Viper.'

'But *you* found us,' I said.

'That's because I had a reason to look,' Avery persisted. 'I only found out your real names recently. What possible reason could McMurdo have for bothering? He's owned the Medusa gene for over fourteen years – he could have used it a hundred times for all we know.'

'Did you see if there are other people with the Medusa gene, Ed?' Ketty asked eagerly.

'No.' Ed's voice rose defensively. 'I keep telling you, I wasn't looking for anything except where McMurdo is hiding Geri's confession.'

'There could be *millions* of us,' Dylan said, wide-eyed.

'Never mind millions,' I snapped. 'I'm only interested in the four of us and how much McMurdo knows about us. Why can't the rest of you stay focused on what's really important?'

There was a tense pause.

'Why are you so worried about this, Nico?' Cal said.

'Yeah, Nico,' Dylan sneered. 'What's with the neurosis? It's like you've morphed into Ed.'

They all laughed. Even Ed.

I shrugged. I wanted to tell the others that McMurdo had seen my face . . . more, that he'd recognised me . . . but that would mean acknowledging I'd slipped up and I couldn't bear the humiliation, especially not in front of Cal.

An hour or so later we were back at Avery's ranch. Ketty and Dylan ran straight off to the swimming pool. I could hear them splashing around with Cal – and shrieking with laughter. Ed was using the Clusterchaos program that Harry had left us to access the layout of the bank we were going to have to break into.

I'd sat with him for a while, watching to see how Clusterchaos worked. A hacker's software program, it basically latched onto whatever search terms you directed it to, slicing through all the encryptions and firewalls put up to protect the information.

It took a while to find the bank data and after thirty minutes or so I left Ed to it and wandered into the Snug. It was empty. I could hear Ketty and Cal, still laughing their heads off.

Why did Ketty like him? I didn't get it. Worse – why

was she choosing to be out at the pool with Cal, instead of in here with me?

I tried not to think about it. I was still worried about McMurdo recognising me. What did that mean? And what would McMurdo do now he knew that I was here in Sydney?

I sat in the Snug, lying at full stretch on one of the white leather sofas with my head resting in my hands. After a while, Philly came past to let me know she was going out to pick up the younger kids from some play date they'd been on, but that Avery was in his study if I needed anything.

I lay quietly for a bit longer. The girls were still in the pool. From the violent splashing noises I could hear, it sounded like Cal was using his Medusa skill to dive-bomb into the water from a great height. Ed was still hunched over the computer in the next room.

My mind kept going back to McMurdo and how on earth he knew who I was. Avery had said that until he'd started searching a few days ago, he hadn't even known our proper names – let alone what we looked like. Why should McMurdo know?

I sat up. I couldn't bear going over it any more. I had to tell Avery what had happened . . . see if he could shed any light on McMurdo's recognition of me.

I set off for Avery's study, which, Philly had explained, was on the first floor at the opposite end of the house from our bedrooms.

I could hear Avery speaking on the phone as I approached. Not wanting to disturb him, I walked quietly to the door and peered into the room. It was large and airy and white-walled – as simple and expensive as everywhere else in the house, with a row of bookshelves and a large leather desk in the corner. Avery was sitting in the swivel chair at the desk, turned to face out of the open window. Though this room was on the opposite side of the house from the pool, the shrieks and yells of the others filled the air. It sounded like an army of people were in the pool.

'It's the kids . . . they're all swimming,' Avery said into the phone. His voice was low and intense. 'Listen, I've got the DNA results on Nico. It's confirmed.' There was a pause while the person on the other end of the phone presumably said something. 'Yes,' Avery went on. 'Father and son.'

I froze, ducking back behind the door. What was he talking about? There was another pause. Avery's back stiffened.

'Right now? Nico doesn't suspect a thing.'

My heart pounded as Avery put down the phone. I could hear his heavy sigh from my position just outside the door.

I tried to process what I'd just heard. Something about a DNA test . . . about a father and son . . . about *me*. Avery had said my name specifically.

Why?

Head spinning, I turned and crept away down the corridor.

13: Going Alone

I stumbled downstairs, careful to make no noise. I could hear Avery pacing about his study as I reached the Snug and sank, head in hands, into a sofa.

He had no idea I'd overheard him.

And I had no idea exactly what I'd overheard.

One thing was certain, though. There was no way now that I could talk to Avery about McMurdo recognising me earlier. In fact, that terrifying moment had been virtually pushed out of my head by Avery's conversation on the phone.

The more I thought about it, the clearer it became . . . Avery had done a DNA test to find out about a father and a son. And he'd referred to me directly, immediately afterwards. I knew about DNA tests – you didn't need much of a person to do the test . . . a strand of hair, a swipe of saliva. With a jolt, I remembered Avery's gaze fixed on my lemonade glass yesterday.

It seemed only logical that I was the son in Avery's test.

But who was the father?

Outside the girls and Cal were still shrieking and splashing away.

'What's up?'

I looked up to see Ed standing over me. He held an open laptop in his arms and had a worried frown on his face.

I shook my head, emotion overwhelming me. There was a huge lump in my throat. I couldn't speak. I looked down at my lap.

Ed sat beside me. 'I've downloaded the floor plans of the bank. It's not going to be easy breaking in – but I've found the best route, I think.' He hesitated. 'Nico, what's the matter?'

I bit hard on my lip. Given the choice, I'd rather have told Ketty first. She always makes me feel better when anything heavy comes up . . . sort of calming and understanding . . . But Ketty was outside with some other boy. And Ed had trusted me earlier. Plus, I knew that, irritating though he could be, Ed was actually the kind of guy who wouldn't take the mickey if you told him something emotional.

I quickly explained what I'd overheard Avery say. As I spoke, I couldn't help but tell Ed that I'd only been going to speak to Avery because of McMurdo recognising me earlier. I felt slightly better to have offloaded the information and, having finished, sat back with a sigh.

Ed thought for a second. 'I didn't see anything about a DNA test when I mind-read Avery, though I wasn't looking for it.'

'Maybe he was hiding it,' I said. 'You said you thought he was capable of creating "mental walls".'

Ed nodded. 'That's true.' He paused. 'Er . . . do you think maybe *McMurdo*'s your dad?'

I stared at him. 'What makes you say that?'

'Well, for a start, it's really odd that McMurdo – who supposedly only knows you by your Medusa name – was able to recognise you, isn't it?'

'Of course it's odd, but still . . .' A shiver slithered down my spine.

Ed shrugged. 'It makes sense for other reasons, too. We know McMurdo worked in London until he came over here. He's a scientist who knew Geri Paterson . . . he certainly knew of William Fox, even if they'd never met . . .'

'But my mum was pregnant before she met the Foxes,' I insisted. 'Fergus introduced her to William.'

'Are you sure?' Ed said. 'Is that what Fergus said? Or just what you assumed? And didn't you tell me once that your mum always refused to talk about who your dad was?'

I nodded. Ed was right. From the little I knew of my mum's life before she had me, it fitted. McMurdo could be my father.

'But why would Avery do a DNA test on me and McMurdo and not tell me about it unless . . .'

'Unless he's somehow double-crossing us over McMurdo?' Ed said. 'Maybe even in league with McMurdo? If I didn't see that he was planning on doing a DNA test on you, he could have hidden anything from me.'

Another shiver snaked down my spine. What was the phrase Avery had used? *Nico doesn't suspect a thing.*

Avery's feet sounded above our heads, walking along the landing towards the stairs. As he descended, he saw us sitting on the sofa.

'Ah, good, there you are,' he said. 'I wanted to tell you that I've just spoken to your stepdad, Nico.'

'Right.' I looked at him suspiciously. If Fergus had really been on the phone, he'd surely have insisted on speaking to me. 'Didn't Fergus want to talk to us?'

'Of course he did, but it wasn't a good line and I thought you were out by the pool.' Avery's face was guarded as usual. I couldn't tell what he was really thinking. 'To be honest, Fergus was a bit shocked to hear from me. We've never spoken before and . . . anyway, he's going to call back later, in an hour or so. We'll be able to contact the other parents then as well.'

'Great,' I said, attempting a smile.

Avery threw me a curious glance. 'Everything okay?'

'Fine,' I said.

'By the way, McMurdo's art gallery has found the paint-ing you teleported behind the radiator. There are a lot of red faces, but the whole thing's being dealt with as a massive mistake. So that's worked out well.' Avery chuck-led. 'Right, I'll tell the girls that they should be able to speak to their folks later tonight.' Avery turned to Ed. 'Any luck hacking into the bank floor plans?'

'Yes,' Ed said.

I nudged his leg, trying to shut him up.

'Er . . . that is, I'm getting there,' Ed went on, his face colouring. 'I just need a bit more time.'

Avery nodded. 'Well, we'll need a couple of days to plan the attack on the bank. Going in on a Sunday is probably the best bet. Obviously, I'll come with you as far as I can.' He went outside.

As he disappeared from view, heading for the pool area, I turned to Ed.

'No way was he talking to Fergus just now,' I said.

Ed gulped. 'I know. He was *definitely* hiding something.'

'Well, whatever he's really doing it's about a lot more than getting the evidence on Geri from McMurdo's safety deposit box.'

'So what do we do now?' Ed asked anxiously.

I met his gaze, my own thoughts firming as I spoke them.

'We get the girls, break into the bank and take the safety deposit box right now,' I said.

Ed's eyes widened. 'But it's not even night-time.'

'We can't afford to wait,' I said. 'We have to find some way of fooling Avery and getting to that bank before he knows what we're doing. Otherwise, we could be walking into a trap.'

'But *how*?'

'We use Cal,' I said. 'We say we want to try flying as a group . . . test it out . . . and we get him to fly us as close to Sydney as he can. Then we dump him and head for the bank.'

'Why not tell him what we're planning?' asked Ed.

'Because if Avery's working against us, then you can bet Cal is, too. Have you seen the way he looks at me?'

Ed nodded. 'He is a bit hostile to you, but then you're a bit hostile to h—'

'You need to contact Ketty and Dylan telepathically,' I interrupted. 'Get them out of that pool and ready to leave while I work out how we're going to break into this bank in broad daylight.'

'I'm sure we can tell Cal what we're planning,' Ketty said. 'We don't have to say we suspect Avery, just that we want to get on with finding the evidence against Geri.'

'No,' I said.

'But I don't like lying, especially to Cal.'

Great.

'We can't risk it,' I snapped. 'Can't you see that?'

Ketty shook her head.

We were waiting for Cal at the gates of the ranch. Dylan and Ketty had accepted that Avery was working behind our backs though, I suspected, more because Ed was saying so than because I was. They'd also both agreed we needed to set off to retrieve the evidence on Geri straight away.

However, neither of them wanted to leave Cal out of the expedition. Dylan's argument was that he'd be useful at the bank. Ketty, on the other hand, seemed more concerned that he'd be upset if we deceived him. Why did she care so much about his feelings?

I looked out at the dusty landscape beyond the ranch. The sun was bright in the sky and the distant outline of the city shimmered in the distance. The blue hills rose up beyond. I still couldn't take in how big everything was.

'We'll be fine without Cal,' I said. 'I mean, we haven't got Amy who'd probably be more useful in terms of getting into the bank and nobody's complaining about that.'

Ketty set her mouth in that grim line I knew so well and turned her face away.

Man, now what had I said?

A minute later Cal joined us.

'So you just want to try flying together?' he said with a frown.

'Yes,' I lied.

'Cool,' Cal said. 'Though I've never taken four people up at once.'

'If it's too many, I'm happy to find another way,' Ed said quickly.

I glared at him.

'Nah, should be fine,' Cal said. 'Especially if we're just gonna have a look round the area.' He hesitated. 'You know we'll have to stay real low in the trees when we get nearer the city. Dad'll kill me if anyone sees us.'

'Well, we wouldn't want you getting in trouble with *Daddy*,' I said. 'Can we get going?'

Cal threw me a contemptuous glance. 'If we rush, we'll make mistakes.'

126

It was the kind of thing Ed would say and sounded as pompous as he often did.

'Fine,' I said sarcastically. 'Please take your time.'

The atmosphere tensed. Cal looked at Ketty.

'What should we do first?' she said.

'Join hands.' Cal organised us so that the two girls were standing on either side of him with me next to Ketty and Ed on Dylan's other side.

'Now I'm not gonna do any acrobatics in the air, so just hold on tight and keep your body as still as you can.'

'Oh,' Ed said, the colour draining from his face. 'Do I really have to do this?'

'Oh yeah, Chino Boy,' Dylan said with a grin. 'You'll be awesome.'

'Everyone needs to follow my lead and do what I say, okay?' Cal said.

He was quite clearly directing those words at me.

'Whatever,' I replied grudgingly.

'Everybody holding on?' asked Cal.

We all nodded our assent. I gripped Ketty's hand tightly. I suddenly realised that I was about to fly. Adrenalin surged through me. But before I had time to think about how exciting it was, my feet had left the ground.

14: Flight

My stomach seemed to fall away as we soared up . . .
up . . . into the air. For a few seconds, I was filled with
terror, gripping Ketty's hand as hard as I could. My mouth
was open, but I was too traumatised to scream. And then
I felt it . . . the flow of energy through Ketty's arm . . .
coming from Cal. It was holding us in the air, like we were
on a surfboard riding the crest of a wave, or in a roller-
coaster just before the deepest plunge.

I kept my feet together. Wind whistled past. I looked
down. Already, the ranch looked like a toy building.

This was, without doubt, the most exhilarating thing I'd
ever done – the total definition of freedom. The ground
raced by beneath me, the wind whooshing in my ears. We
rose and fell a fraction.

'Isn't it amazing!' Ketty yelled over the noise of the
rushing wind.

I stared at her. No wonder she loved this. I gazed past
her at Cal. He was clearly working hard to steer us. All his

movements were precise and controlled, yet he moved with effortless grace . . . his face utterly focused.

A stab of envy pierced me. I'd always thought I had the best Medusa gift – telekinesis – but, at that moment, I would have given anything to be able to do what Cal could do . . . to be the one making Ketty's eyes shine.

But it was him.

On his other side, Dylan looked like she was whooping with pleasure, though I couldn't hear anything over the noise of the wind rushing past my ears. Beside her, Ed's mouth was open in a scream – though whether one of terror or delight I couldn't tell.

Cal dropped lower and I had that delicious, theme-park-ride experience of leaving my stomach several metres above me as I fell. I grinned. It was impossible not to, as we rose and dipped again. Cal steered us to the left, away from a long stretch of road and into a huge wood. He flew us through the trees until they became too densely packed for us to pass safely, then he landed.

We came in slowly, but even so I stumbled as I touched the ground again. Ketty, landing gracefully beside me, tugged at my hand to stop me from falling over completely.

I turned to her. 'Wow,' I said.

Ketty flung her arms round me. 'I knew you'd love it,' she said breathlessly, drawing back to look me in the eyes. Her face was lit up, her natural prettiness heightened by the pink flush in her cheeks. 'Isn't it the coolest thing?'

For a second, all I could see was her excited expression,

then I got a sense of the others around us in the cool shade of the trees. Ed was sitting on a tree stump, his face a nasty shade of green. Dylan was bent over, talking to him. But Cal was watching me and Ketty. He'd heard her question and was waiting for my answer.

I raised my voice slightly to make sure he heard.

'Flying was okay,' I said, 'but I've been on cooler rides at millions of theme parks.'

Ketty flinched as if I'd hit her. She jumped back, away from me, a hurt look in her eyes.

I looked again at Cal. He was breathing heavily, his face glistening with sweat. He shrugged.

'That was hard work,' he said. 'I'm sorry you didn't like it.'

Ketty rushed over to him. 'It was brilliant,' she said.

She hugged him. Jealousy wriggled through me like a snake. Cal put his arms round her, then looked up at me. He raised his eyebrows, triumphant.

I stared from him to Ketty, knowing that I'd been rude, but with no idea what to do to make things right . . . to make Ketty see I wasn't mean and difficult, like she'd said.

'Which way's Sydney?' Dylan asked, turning round from Ed.

Cal pointed through the trees. 'Though it's only the very outskirts,' he said.

Ketty disentangled herself from his hug. She didn't look at me.

'Are you okay, Ed?' she said, her voice filled with concern.

Ed nodded, his face still unnaturally pale and tinged with green.

'I don't think I'm going to be sick now,' he said.

Dylan rolled her eyes. 'Awesome,' she said. 'Did you hear him screaming? Right in my ear!'

We set off through the wood. Soon the spaces between the trees became so narrow we could only walk single file. Cal led the way, followed by Ketty. I was last.

After another twenty minutes we reached the street. A hundred metres or so along the road were a few shops and a bus stop where we were planning on getting a bus to the city centre. Cal told us the name of the place, but I barely heard him. Ketty still hadn't looked at me . . . hadn't come near me, in fact, since our flight had ended.

The sun was low in the sky now and a cool breeze whipped through the trees behind us, making me shiver.

'What d'you wanna do now?' Cal said.

'Let's head for that diner,' I said, pointing to a café along the road just beside the bus stop.

This stage of the plan was critical. We had to wait and keep our eyes open for a bus so that when one came, we could make a speedy exit – hopping on the bus before Cal realised what was happening.

As we strolled down the street, Ketty hung back, waiting till I caught up with her. She wasn't smiling.

'Change of plan,' she said. 'We're not leaving Cal behind. Dylan and Ed agree.'

'No way.' Anger rose up in me. 'That's stupid, Ketty.

We don't know if we can trust him. He's Avery Jones's son.'

'Well, Harry is Jack Linden's son and we trusted him.'

'Only after Ed mind-read him.'

'Ed's mind-read Cal again, too.'

I stared at her. 'When did that happen?'

'Earlier. Dylan said we shouldn't tell you yet, but I'm fed up of all of us having to work around your ego.' She threw me a withering look. 'Cal can be useful. He wants to help. Ed says we can trust him. He's in.'

Ketty marched off. Furious, I sped up, trying to reach her, but as I passed Ed, he telepathically pushed his way into my head.

Er, Nico . . . ?

What?

I'm certain Cal doesn't know if Avery is doing stuff behind our backs.

Get out of my head.

Ed vanished and I stomped along, head down.

We reached the diner. Everyone else went inside, but I stayed out on the pavement. My shadow cast a long oval across the road. For a moment, I considered going to the bank on my own. But even as the idea occurred to me, I knew that it was impossible. I'd seen the floor plans and the security protocols. No way could I get into the room with the safety deposit box on my own. I needed the others.

I kicked at the wall of the diner then went inside.

Ketty, Cal, Ed and Dylan were sipping milkshakes in

one of the booths. They looked up as I walked over. I folded my arms and took a deep breath.

'Okay, Cal can come,' I said.

Ed smiled. Dylan rolled her eyes. Cal offered me a smug grin.

I glanced at Ketty. She was staring down at her lap. Irritation raced through me.

'But you stick close to me, Cal, okay?' I said.

Cal nodded. 'Sure, boss,' he said sarcastically.

I checked the road through the window. A bus marked *City Centre* was trundling along the street towards our stop.

'Finish your drinks,' I said. 'We're off.'

15: Bank Job

I sat on my own at the back of the bus. Dylan was in front of me, next to Cal. Ketty had positioned herself in the seat in front of them, next to Ed.

As the bus turned a corner onto a busier street, Cal turned round.

'I don't get it,' he said. 'I mean, I know that you're planning on getting into the bank and I know why you want this safety deposit box, but why are we going now without a full briefing or back-up from Avery?'

Dylan raised her eyebrows. Ed and Ketty stopped talking and looked around too. I cleared my throat.

'Ed and I have sorted everything we need to know – so no need for a briefing. And I'm sorry if you'd feel happier with back-up from Daddy, but we're used to operating on our own.'

Cal's face turned scarlet. Ketty's angry glare burned my cheeks. Ed shook his head. I sat back in my seat and gazed out of the window. Who cared what they all thought.

After twenty minutes of awkward silence we reached the bank.

'Any visions, Ketts?' I asked, trying to keep my voice light.

She shook her head, making eye contact with me for the first time since before the diner. 'I'm too stressed to see anything,' she snapped. 'Which is totally your fault.'

Don't blame me, they're your powers. I bit back the words.

'We'll be fine without the precog,' Dylan said impatiently. 'Let's just get going.'

I nodded. 'Wait here. I'm going inside to see how it looks.'

I put my sunglasses on and kept my head bowed as I opened the door into the bank.

It was large and intimidatingly smart, with an atmosphere of hushed formality. The foyer felt cold after the heat of the street. A blast of air con sent a shiver across the back of my neck.

The woman at the help desk just to the left of the entrance looked up at me suspiciously. I kept my head down. No way was I making the same mistake here that I had at the art gallery.

Beyond her the bank was quiet. Just a small knot of people around the paying-in machines and a couple standing with a teller. There was only one security guard, but unfortunately, he was standing close to the staff door that was our route through to the bank vault containing the safety deposit boxes. I left the bank.

'There's hardly anyone in there,' I said, trotting down the steps to where the others waited outside on the pavement.

'That's good, isn't it?' Cal said.

'Not really,' I snapped. 'It means fewer distractions for the bank workers so they're more likely to spot us.'

'No one's gonna spot us,' Dylan drawled. 'Not if you take care of the security cameras.'

'Ed has to take care of the security guard by the staff door first,' I said, giving him a nudge. 'Go on,' I urged. 'Inside.'

Ed gave a business-like nod, then vanished inside. We stood on the pavement, waiting. Our plan followed the same procedure that we'd used many times before. Ed would use his newly-honed hypnosis skills to ensure no one stopped us as we passed through the locked door that led along the corridor to the bank vault. The rest was up to me and, if we were attacked, to Dylan as well.

I glanced at Ketty. We all knew that, of the four of us standing outside, Ed was most likely to contact her tele-pathically when he was ready.

'Not yet,' she said.

Suddenly Cal jerked his head up. 'Whoa!' His eyes widened. 'Ed's inside my mind.'

I frowned. Why was Ed communicating with *Cal*?

'That's nice,' Dylan said with a sarky smile. 'Ed's trying to make you feel like you're part of the group.'

'What's he saying?' asked Ketty.

'He's saying he's mind-read the security guy and planted the idea that its okay for us to walk through the staff door.'

I tugged my hood over my head. 'Let's go.'

As I entered the bank a second time, it occurred to me just how amazing Ed's mind-reading talent was . . . and how far he had developed it in such a short time. From basic telepathy to an ability to manipulate other people's thoughts was a massive achievement, not that Ed ever made a big deal of it.

He was waiting by the door. He glanced around the bank, waving his hand to indicate the security guard by the staff door across the lobby.

'He's expecting us to walk through that door in the next few minutes, then he'll forget we were ever here,' he said. 'I haven't hurt him or even looked beyond the surface layer of his thoughts.'

'Thanks, Ed,' I said. 'That's brilliant.'

Ed's face reddened with pride.

'Come on.' Dylan pointed at a couple of customers now walking out of the bank. 'Let's go while it's quiet.'

We crossed the lobby. As we neared the security guard, I looked around for the security camera I knew would be trained on the staff door behind him.

There. It was positioned on the opposite wall, just below the ceiling. I twisted my wrist, intending to turn the camera so that the lens pointed away from the door.

The camera didn't budge. I stopped . . . tried again . . . nothing.

My heart raced. I could feel the others watching me. I raised my hand higher this time, focusing harder on the arm of the camera that protruded from the wall. Why wouldn't it move?

'What's wrong?' Dylan hissed in my ear.

'The camera's stuck,' I said.

'We have to move it,' said Ed, his voice rising with anxiety. 'We can't risk anyone seeing us going inside.'

I tried again. The camera refused to move.

'What are we going to do?' Ketty asked.

The blood throbbed in my temples. If the camera wouldn't move, I had to think of another way to prevent it from filming us.

'I'm going to cover the lens,' I said.

I glanced around the room. My eyes fell on a pile of papers on the front desk. If I could get the street door to fly open at the right moment, I could make it look as if a gust of wind blew into the bank and sent the papers flying into the air. As soon as I thought this, I acted.

In one flowing movement, I opened the door telekinetically and teleported the papers into the air. People turned around, their mouths agape at the disturbance.

I kept my focus on a single sheet of paper, lifting it higher and higher until it was positioned over the camera lens.

'Come on!' I breathed.

The five of us raced over to the staff door. We needn't have worried about the security guard; he was transfixed by the papers still swirling in the air.

I focused on the lock. A swift flick of my hand and the security bar sprang open.

Dylan and Cal raced through the door. Ed and Ketty stopped. Our plan was for them to wait in the lobby for us to return, ready to send a warning telepathically if need be.

As I passed Ketty, we looked into each other's eyes. I wanted to say something . . . to put our earlier row behind us . . . but I had no idea what. Anyway, there was no time.

'Go,' she whispered.

And, with a final twist of my hand to release all the papers still soaring about the bank lobby, I followed Cal and Dylan through the door. It shut behind me with a snap.

We were in a long corridor. Doors led off on either side, but from the plans we'd seen earlier, the vault with the safety deposit box we were looking for was right at the end.

We flew along the carpet, round a corner to the left. I spotted another security camera up ahead. This one turned easily when I focused on it.

We ran, silently, past an open office. Neither of the workers inside the small room noticed us. Seconds later we reached a sturdy locked door. I opened it using telekinesis. No problem. Behind it stood the vault. The opening was arched and made from metal. It was a harder lock for me to get past, but I was confident I could do it.

I stood facing the vault, both arms outstretched,

visualising how it would look from the inside. I'd learned some time back that you don't need to be able to see the lock in precise detail in order to open it . . . but you do have to see it as a whole.

Seconds ticked by. Dylan paced backwards and forwards, the flick of her red ponytail just in my eyeline.

'What's holding us up?' Cal said desperately.

'Shut up,' I snapped.

I could hear him muttering to himself. Then Dylan's whispered drawl. She was presumably telling him that I needed time to get the vault door open.

I redoubled my efforts. At last the four vault locks released as one and the three of us ran inside the vault. It was a small room, one wall of which was lined with tiny cubicles.

'Look for safety deposit box 1763,' I reminded the others.

We raced up and down the lines. My heart thudded. We hadn't heard from Ed yet – which had to mean the coast was still clear. But every second we spent in here, we were taking a terrible risk.

'Here it is!' Cal pointed at one of the cubicles. He turned to me expectantly. 'It's locked.'

Another flick of my wrist and the cubicle popped open. Cal drew the handle back. Six boxes were stacked inside. He pulled them out.

'Here,' he said.

He handed safety deposit box 1763 to Dylan who set it

on the table in the middle of the room. It was made of chrome and about the size of a shoebox.

I bent over the electronic keyholes and punched in the entry code Ed had mind-read from McMurdo, trying to shut out the hushed tension of the room and the sound of my own frantic heartbeat.

I took a deep breath. I could feel Dylan beside me, peering anxiously over my shoulder. We were about to get our hands on the film of Geri Paterson's confession . . . the evidence that would enable us to expose Geri, clear our names and go home.

I reached down and lifted the lid of the box.

For a second, there was silence as Dylan and I stared inside, unable to believe what we were seeing.

And then the room filled with noise as the bank's security alarm pierced the air.

16: Inside the Box

The box was empty apart from a piece of white card. I stared at it, the alarm screaming around me, as the vault door slammed shut.

'No!' Dylan raced across the room.

Five words were written in black ink: *Better luck next time, Nico!*

My heart plummeted to my shoes. This whole thing had been a trap.

'Nico!' Dylan yelled. 'Open the vault door!'

I looked up, trying to focus on the door. I raised my hands, but I couldn't concentrate. Blood pounded in my ears. My whole body was shaking.

The noise of the alarm pierced through my skull. Beside me, Cal was yelling.

I closed my eyes, trying to steady my breath . . . to calm down.

'Come on, Nico!' Dylan shouted.

I opened my eyes and, taking a long breath from deep

inside my stomach, I gave it everything I had. It worked. The door slid open.

Dylan, already right beside it, raced outside. Cal and I ran after her. Back down the corridor. Bank personnel were milling about, all talking at the tops of their voices. A security guard – gun in outstretched arm – lunged into the corridor ahead of us.

'Stop!' he yelled.

Dylan stopped instantly, flinging her arms wide to protect me and Cal. Her hand gripped my arm and I felt the energy of her force field flow around me, just as it had outside the explosion at Wardingham a few days ago.

She turned, her eyes wild.

'Run!' she shrieked.

The three of us pounded down the corridor.

'Stop or I'll shoot!' the guard yelled.

'Keep going!' Dylan shouted.

We ran on. I darted sideways, through an open door into an empty storeroom, momentarily losing Dylan's hand on my arm.

Behind us the guard fired a shot into the ceiling. I jumped.

'He missed,' Cal hissed. 'It's okay.'

We raced through the storeroom, into an office. I was leading the way, following the open doors. But I had no idea where I was going . . . or how on earth we were going to get out of this bank.

Nico . . . where are . . . ? All of a sudden Ed appeared in my head.

Not now, I thought-spoke.

Ed vanished.

And then a man dressed in a black T-shirt and jeans, a mask pulled over his face, lurched in front of us. I raised my hands, ready to haul him out of our way, but to my surprise the man stepped back, pointing ahead of him down the corridor.

I blinked, taking in what he was showing us. A few metres along the wall was a small hole – about the size of a large pet flap. The man pointed again, then raced to the hole. He tugged at a crumbling piece of brick. I bent down. The hole led outside – into daylight.

'Through here,' he said, his voice muffled by the mask over his mouth.

Behind us another shot fired. I didn't hesitate. I scrambled through the hole and stood up. The sun glared in my eyes. I could just make out that we were in a car park.

I felt a hand on my arm. The man in the mask led me past the cars to a van parked just a couple of metres away.

'In the back,' he ordered.

'Wait!' I looked around.

Dylan and Cal were beside me, looking as alarmed as I felt.

'Who are you?' I demanded.

The alarm was still shrieking out of the bank. In the distance we could hear police sirens.

'There's no time,' the man said. His voice was still muffled, but I was certain I didn't know him.

'No.' I raised my hands.

Instantly, the man whipped out a small can. He pressed the top and an odourless liquid squirted out. A fine spray coated all three of us, hitting me right in the face.

I blinked, shocked, then raised my hand to teleport the can away. But as soon as I tried, I knew that my telekinesis had gone. All the psychic power had drained out of me like water out of a leaking bucket.

My heart raced.

The man opened the back of the van and jerked his head to indicate we should get inside.

I glanced at Dylan. From her expression I was guessing that she was experiencing the same block on her abilities that I was.

The man pocketed his spray can and took out a gun. 'I'm not asking again.'

I tried to jerk the gun out of his hand.

It didn't work. I had no idea what was happening. But I could see we had no choice.

I hauled myself into the back of the van. Dylan and Cal followed right after me. I turned as the man slammed the door shut. As soon as we were inside, I tried to open it telekinetically. Nothing happened.

As the van's engine roared into life, I turned to Dylan.

'I've lost my Medusa power.'

'Me too.' Her eyes were wide and desperate. 'I can't protect myself.'

The horror of this filled me as the van screeched round

a corner. My eyes were getting used to the darkness. The back of the van was completely empty.

Cal was backed into a corner, his head in his hands. Suddenly I was sure Cal was behind everything that had happened.

'I *knew* we shouldn't have told you what we were planning.' I lunged across the van and hurled myself at him. 'What have you done?'

I shoved Cal in the chest. He stumbled backwards.

'I didn't do anything,' he gasped. 'This guy's got me, too. I can't *fly*. Why would I do that to myself?'

'He's right, Nico, think it through,' said Dylan.

I staggered backwards, panting for breath. I sat down, bent over my knees, my head in my hands.

If Cal was telling the truth, then who had taken us?

Why was the film of Geri's confession no longer in that safety deposit box?

And what on earth had happened to our psychic abilities?

Another ten minutes or so passed. We barely spoke, all three of us in shock. And then the van stopped with a jolt.

A second later the back door opened. The man, still wearing his mask, beckoned us out. I reached out my hands, trying to move him telekinetically.

Again, nothing happened.

I jumped down, feelings of frustration and fear shooting through me.

The van was parked outside a small detached house. I glanced down the street. A copse of trees opposite, then more houses in the distance. Maybe we could make a run for it.

'Don't think about it, Nico.' The man had followed my gaze.

As I turned towards him, he brandished his gun, then pointed towards a door in the side of the house. I followed Cal and Dylan through, along a short corridor and into a small, stuffy room.

No furniture. No windows

The four of us stood in silence for a second.

'Who are you?' I said.

The man pulled off his mask.

He looked straight at me. 'You know who I am, Nico. You saw me the other day. I just left you a note in my safety deposit box.'

I stared back at him. He was right. A million questions flooded my head. But before I could ask any of them, the man smiled, his dark brown eyes crinkling as his gaze shifted from me to the others.

'Dylan . . . Cal . . . we haven't met, but the pleasure is mine,' he said in a crisp English accent. 'I'm Rod McMurdo.'

17: The Deal

The whitewashed room McMurdo had brought us into was completely bare. Cal and Dylan stood on either side of me.

'What do you want?' I demanded.

McMurdo drew the white card with the words *Better luck next time, Nico!* from out of my pocket.

'I want you to do something for me, Nico,' he said. 'That's why I saved you back at the bank.'

'How did you even know we'd be there?' I said, glancing suspiciously at Cal.

'After I saw you outside the art gallery earlier I sent a security guard to follow you.'

'He *saw* you?' Dylan turned on me accusingly.

I kept my eyes on McMurdo, who smiled.

'Didn't Nico mention it?' he said lightly. 'Well, anyway, the guard followed you as far as Avery Jones's car. He saw you all drive off together. There are two others, aren't there – a boy and a girl?'

I stared at him. No way was I giving away any

information about Ketty or Ed. I glanced sideways at Cal and Dylan. They looked as determined to keep silent as I was.

'Ah, well,' McMurdo went on. 'So there you all were with Avery Jones and I started wondering what Avery could possibly want with me after all this time. So I did a little investigation into what's been going on in England and – to cut a long story short – after an hour or so I realised you must be after my film of Geri Paterson's confession to murder. Since then, I've been keeping a watch on the bank where the film was hidden, taking care to remove it first, of course.' He smiled again. 'One thing still mystifies me – how did you know for sure where it was? Did you use your Medusa abilities? I mean, that safety deposit box you got into . . . the number was never written down and I never told anyone. Is one of you a telepath of some kind?'

I stared at him.

'None of *us* can read minds,' Dylan snapped.

McMurdo shrugged. 'Well, perhaps one of the others can. Anyway, his work is impressive.'

I made a small movement with my hands, attempting to teleport McMurdo off the floor. It was no good. My telekinesis was totally gone.

'You're stopping us using our abilities,' I said.

'That's right.' McMurdo nodded. 'The spray I used on you contains a chemical called Medutox that prevents the neural pathways linked to your Medusa powers from firing. I'm releasing it into this room, too – you're breathing it

149

right now. Don't worry, its effects will wear off once you're no longer exposed.'

So that was why I couldn't move anything with my mind and why Dylan had lost her force field and Cal could no longer fly.

With a jolt, I realised that it also explained why Ed had not made remote telepathic contact since we'd been shut inside the van. He was probably trying . . . but we were unable to hear him.

'So, if you've created some antidote, then you admit Geri Paterson sold you the Medusa gene?' Dylan said, tight-lipped.

McMurdo looked at her. 'Ah, Dylan . . . I've often wondered if I would ever meet you. I've always felt terrible that the Medusa gene robbed you not just of your beautiful mother, like the others, but your father, too.'

'I don't care how you feel.' Dylan crossed her arms. 'You took the gene code from Geri even though you knew she'd murdered both my parents. You're no better than she is.'

'Excuse me, but I disagree,' McMurdo said patiently. 'Geri gave me the gene code because your dad . . . William Fox . . . was . . . er, a difficult man to deal with and she thought I might be more amenable. She was in a hurry . . . She hadn't had time to copy the gene code, not that she would have understood any of its references. Geri is not a scientist.' He paused. 'She gave me the code because I'd promised to work for her, but when she realised I had no intention of doing so, she wanted the gene code back. Naturally, I refused. I mean, I had Geri's confession on film – evidence she killed William and Ashley Fox. It was a stalemate, so Geri left.'

'What have you done with the film of her confession?' Dylan demanded.

McMurdo jerked his head to indicate the rest of the house. 'It's here,' he said. 'It's safe.' He hesitated. 'I didn't know at the time that using the Medusa gene would result in the deaths of the mothers who carried the Medusa babies. I think, looking back, that Geri didn't tell me deliberately – as a sort of revenge for double-crossing her.'

'So you used the gene on me,' Cal said furiously. 'You persuaded my dad to let you experiment on me?'

'Both your parents agreed to give it a try,' McMurdo said. 'None of us thought anyone would suffer as a result. I didn't use it again. Not on a real person. Unlike Avery, I've never been interested in the developmental effects of the gene. Only in controlling it.'

'What does that mean?' I said.

'My ambition was never to raise a child who would one day exhibit psychic abilities of some kind. My aim was to harness the ability and make it available to a wider market.'

'You mean like invent a kind of Medusa pill people could take?' Dylan said.

'Yes, like a drug that temporarily gives you a psychic power.'

'And has it worked?' I held my breath. What McMurdo

151

was describing would be huge if it happened. People could just pop a pill and find themselves able to read minds or see into the future or move objects telekinetically.

'No so far.' McMurdo sighed. 'Though I accidentally discovered the Medutox I used on you, that *prevents* the gene from working.'

McMurdo left us for a few hours. We kept testing our Medusa powers. They seemed to return briefly a couple of times, then went again. Eventually McMurdo returned. He explained he'd been testing exactly how long it took for the drug he'd sprayed us with to wear off.

'You said you wanted me to do something for you?' I said.

'That's right,' McMurdo said. 'There's a man who needs dealing with . . .'

'A man?' I said.

'My work on the Medusa gene – then developing Medutox – hasn't been cheap,' said McMurdo. 'I have debts.'

'Why is that our problem?' Dylan snarled.

'I owe this particular man a lot of money,' McMurdo said.

'So?' I said. 'I don't have any money. None of us do.'

McMurdo laughed. 'I'm not expecting you to pay him off.'

'So what do you want me to do?'

McMurdo fixed me with a serious look. 'I want you to kill him.'

There was a stunned silence. He couldn't be serious.

'You're genuinely asking me to take somebody's life?' I said finally.

'Yes.' McMurdo nodded. 'You can take either Cal or Dylan with you to help. The other one stays here as collateral. If you even think about double-crossing me, they'll die, too.'

My thoughts raced back to the suspicions I'd had earlier. Was this why McMurdo had recognised me before . . . because he'd been planning on using me all along? What about the DNA test results conversation I'd overheard Avery having on the telephone?

I stared at McMurdo. 'Why me?' I said. 'When I saw you outside the gallery, you knew who I was and now you want me to go on this mission for you. Why me?'

'Because you're special, Nico,' McMurdo said.

'Special?' I made sure my voice sounded cold and cynical, but inside my guts twisted into a knot. Was McMurdo about to announce that I was his son?

'Yes,' he said. 'I've kept tabs on you and your ability since it first came to light a few months ago. That's how I recognised you. Telekinesis is an amazing and powerful skill.'

My heart thudded. Was that really it?

'Does Avery know about your work?' Dylan asked.

'No.' McMurdo looked genuinely shocked.

'And you seriously want to send Nico to kill some gangster?' Dylan demanded.

153

'Yes. I'll explain the full situation in a minute,' McMurdo said. 'You can decide how to approach the task while we're on the way.'

'I'm not killing anyone for you,' I said, trying to keep my voice steady.

'Then you will die . . . and so will Cal and Dylan.'

McMurdo's voice was completely unemotional. I didn't doubt for a second that he meant what he said. Surely this man couldn't be my father?

'How can I do what you're asking without having my Medusa power back?' I said.

'I told you the effects of the Medutox will wear off,' McMurdo said. 'But make no mistake, if you attempt to double-cross me, the person left behind will die. Now which one of these two do you want to take with you?'

'I can't choose,' I said. 'You can't make me do this.'

McMurdo cocked his gun. 'We don't have time for hissy fits, Nico. Pick either Cal or Dylan . . . or I pick one of them for you . . .'

I glanced desperately from Cal to Dylan. I had no idea exactly what I would be required to do . . . I could barely get my head around the idea that McMurdo was attempting to force me to kill someone, let alone how he expected me to do it . . .

Whatever . . . I tried to focus on which one of the two others would be most helpful in aiding our escape.

Dylan would be useful because once her force field was engaged she couldn't be harmed. Yet McMurdo had a

154

fail-safe way of undoing that force field – which made Dylan's gift redundant.

Cal, on the other hand, could fly. Once he was out of range of McMurdo's antidote, he'd be able to make his way back to Avery and tell the others where we were. I weighed the risks of Cal betraying me. They were surely low. Yes, the more I thought about it, the more certain I was that whatever Avery had meant when he said: *Nico doesn't suspect a thing* . . . neither he nor Cal had anything to do with McMurdo's trap.

'Hurry up, Nico,' McMurdo said. 'Choose.'

'I'll take Cal,' I said.

I looked at Dylan, trying to communicate that I would come back . . . that I wasn't abandoning her.

She nodded her understanding – a fierce jerk of the head.

'Right,' McMurdo said. 'Let's go.'

A few minutes later Cal and I had been bundled into the darkness of the back of the van and we were off again.

We sat in silence as the horror of our situation fell heavily on me. My choice was simple. Kill – or die.

What on earth was I going to do?

18: The Hit

I spent most of the journey discussing the options for escape in a low voice with Cal. We agreed that whatever happened, as soon as Cal was free from the influence of the Medutox, he should fly back to Avery, Ed and Ketty and sound the alarm. Hopefully, the police would be able to reach Dylan before McMurdo. As for me . . . I'd just have to take my chances.

After we'd talked everything through, there was a heavy pause.

'Hey, Nico?' Cal said. He hesitated.

'What?' I said.

'I was kinda surprised that you chose to bring me instead of Dylan on this mission,' he said.

I shrugged. 'I just thought you'd be able to get away easier than her.'

Cal nodded. I got the distinct impression there was something else he wanted to say, but the moment passed and a minute later McMurdo brought the van to a halt.

It was dark outside. As McMurdo opened the back doors, light from a nearby street lamp flooded across his face. I could see the anxiety in his eyes.

We were in a busy street, presumably somewhere in Sydney, though it didn't look like the smart areas I'd seen before. The buildings were set close together – a collection of shops and bars and diners. People were spilling out of doors . . . talking loudly, laughing, arguing. It felt rough and hard, like the sort of area Fergus was forever telling me to avoid at all costs.

'So who's the target?' I said.

McMurdo held up his phone. It showed a picture of a man – much younger than I'd expected – with a flat-top haircut and a gold necklace showing under his open-necked shirt.

'Dan Keirnan – known locally as Diamond,' McMurdo explained. 'He's got fingers in lots of pies . . . gambling rackets mostly.'

'Is that why you owe him money?' Cal said. 'From gambling?'

'It doesn't matter how or why I owe Diamond,' McMurdo snapped. 'All you two need to know is that this is the only way left to deal with the problem. Diamond's no hero. You won't be taking the life of an innocent man.'

I swallowed. 'How exactly are you expecting me to . . . to kill him?'

McMurdo shrugged. 'There are lots of options. He'll have a gun. All his gang have guns . . . and knives. Just take one and use it with your telekinesis. Cal can help.'

I stared at him. Did he seriously think I was capable of handling a gun or a knife . . . and using it in cold blood?

'Remember,' McMurdo said, 'if you double-cross me, then Dylan dies *and* I will track you down and kill you.'

'Why don't you just kill Diamond yourself?' I said.

'I wouldn't get near him. You probably won't either – his men will see you and capture you. But that's kind of the point.'

'What d'you mean?' I said.

'If you get captured, you'll be taken to Dan Kiernan. Then you can use your telekinesis to find a way to kill him.'

I shook my head. This was the craziest mission I'd ever been sent on. Cal and I had no idea exactly how many people we were up against and, once we reached our target, I was supposed to do the most extreme thing possible to him – and get away afterwards.

Except . . . it struck me that Cal and I getting safely out after the murder wasn't part of McMurdo's plan at all. As far as I could see, the chances of that happening were between low and impossible. Not that McMurdo cared. He just wanted someone to do his dirty work for him.

'Time to go,' McMurdo said. He pointed to one of the smarter looking bars a few metres down the road. It was called The Diamond.

'That's Dan's bar,' McMurdo said. 'He'll be in the back room probably . . . It's where he does a lot of his business.'

'How long do we have before the Medutox wears off and we get our Medusa abilities back?' I said.

McMurdo checked his watch. 'Just another couple of minutes. Now *go*.'

There was clearly no point talking any further. Cal and I set off along the street. We passed several groups of people as we walked – men and women clearly focused on having a good night out.

My heart beat fast. I wished more than anything that Ketty was here. Not that I wanted to put her in danger, but her presence always made me feel calmer – and I was certain she would have had a practical suggestion about what we should do now. As it was, I was certain of only one thing.

'I'm not killing this Diamond guy,' I hissed as we neared The Diamond bar.

'I know,' Cal said. 'We have to find some way of getting away without McMurdo seeing us.'

I glanced over my shoulder. McMurdo was leaning against his van, his dark eyes fixed intently on us.

'He's watching,' I said. 'I think we should go inside the bar and head straight for the back door . . . or find some side window we can jump out of. If he thinks we're inside, it'll buy us enough time to rescue Dylan then get back to Avery, Ketty and Ed.'

Cal nodded. His face was very pale.

We reached the front door of The Diamond. Through the glass window I could make out a mass of people inside. 'Looks crowded,' I said.

'That's good,' Cal said. 'It should be easier to slip away without anyone noticing.'

I held out my hand to test my telekinesis on the door. It opened easily. Well, at least I had my Medusa power back.

I followed Cal through the open door. The bar wasn't just busy, it was noisy . . . full of people – mostly in their twenties, I was guessing – sipping drinks and chatting loudly. The music, one of those old-style mixes, dipped and soared in the background. The bar area itself was full of glass and metal, with chairs and tables set in small groups across the floor.

We stood at the door. No one appeared to have noticed our arrival, though it struck me that if we weren't careful, we might be stopped and asked for ID.

Cal pointed to a corridor that led off the bar at the end of the room. It looked like our best bet for finding a way out of the building that wasn't overlooked by the street – where McMurdo was waiting for us.

I headed towards the corridor, my spirits lifting slightly. Maybe this wouldn't be so hard after all. I mean, we just needed to get to a fire door or a toilet with a window . . . anything that would take us outside again.

We reached the corridor. I kept my head down and my walk at stroll-speed, trying not to draw attention to myself. Cal did the same thing.

The men's toilet door was clearly marked just a few metres up ahead. Cal had clocked it, too. I sped up just a fraction. We were almost there.

A hand slammed down on my shoulder.

'Gotcha,' said a deep, male Australian voice.

Rough hands pushed me round to face the man who had caught me. My heart pounded. The man stared at me, his sunburnt face shiny in the dim corridor light.

'Stone me, they're just kids,' he exclaimed to another man, walking towards us.

My heart sank. I glanced at Cal. He looked as terrified as I felt.

The second man reached us. He was small and wiry with mean, dark eyes.

'What are you doing here?' he barked. 'We saw you with that creep McMurdo outside . . . he's got two days left to pay . . . Has he sent you in with Diamond's money?'

I shook my head.

'Then what were you doing with him?' the first man asked. 'And why are you in here?'

I opened my mouth, determined to deny all knowledge of McMurdo, but before I could speak Cal was talking.

'We've come to see Diamond,' he said, his voice strained with anxiety. 'McMurdo sent us with a message.'

What on earth was he doing? I flashed a furious glance at him.

'We need to see Diamond,' Cal hissed under his breath. 'It's our only chance.'

Man, he was suggesting we tried to talk our way out of the situation. From the hard look of his henchmen, I very much doubted Diamond would be prepared to listen.

Cal turned to the sunburnt guard. 'We want to talk to Diamond,' he said.

The guard raised his eyebrows.

'You boys wanna talk to Diamond?' he said. 'Well, isn't that handy . . . cos he *really* wants to talk to you.'

19: Diamond

If the ground-floor corridor had been gloomy, the stairs to the basement were barely visible beneath my feet. The stone steps got darker and darker as we descended. I felt my way along the wall – it was made of bare brick: rough and cold.

I shivered as we reached a black door. Light glimmered underneath it and round the sides. Beside me, Cal trembled.

I'd considered using my telekinesis, but in this darkness I couldn't be sure of getting rid of both the guns trained on us before the men holding them fired.

One of our guards rapped on the door three times and a gruff voice barked at us to enter. As the door swung open, I strained to see past the bright light inside. The room we were ushered into was some kind of office – all black and chrome furniture with splashes of purple in the wall hangings and cushions. A naked light bulb hung low from the centre of the ceiling, the only – incongruously – bleak element in the room.

One guard had stayed outside. The other stood beside me as I peered past the brightness of that central light bulb, searching for the person who'd called to us to enter. He was sitting in a chrome-backed armchair in the far corner of the room. I recognised him straight away: Diamond.

He stood up and walked towards us. He was shorter than I was expecting – only a few centimetres or so taller than me and Cal – and dressed in an open-necked shirt similar to the one in the picture McMurdo had shown us. His hair was neatly gelled and he wore a heavy gold chain round his neck. A diamond earring glittered in his right ear.

He narrowed his sharp eyes as he took us both in.

'So McMurdo sent you.' His accent was strongly Australian. 'D'you have my money?'

'No, sir,' Cal blurted out.

I shot him a look, trying to communicate that he needed to shut up and let me do the talking, but Cal's eyes were fixed on Diamond's face.

Diamond nodded at our guard, who pressed his gun against Cal's temple. I gulped. Diamond turned to me.

'Let's cut to the chase,' he said, a tight sound to his voice. 'Tell me why you're here or your mate gets it.'

I thought fast. Now my telekinesis had come back and we were in a brightly lit room, it should be perfectly possible for me to disarm the guard with the gun, knock out Diamond *and* get Cal and me past the other henchman who was still outside the room.

I focused my attention on the guard's gun and twisted

164

my hand. The weapon teleported easily out of the man's hand, clattering to the floor.

As the guard, a shocked expression on his face, took a step towards it, I lifted him a fraction off his feet so that he tripped and fell.

Open-mouthed, Diamond stared at him.

I grabbed Cal's arm. 'Run!' I yelled.

In seconds we were through the door. Arm outstretched, I teleported the man standing guard in the corridor up in the air. With a wave of my hand, I flung him against the wall. He slumped down. I ran past, Cal at my heels.

'There!' Cal pointed at the fire door at the end of the corridor. It was only a few metres away. We could reach it. We *would* reach it. Just another three seconds.

Two.

One.

Telekinetic energy flowed out of me towards the door . . . the bar pressed down . . . I reached out with my hands to push it open.

And then a shot fired behind me and Cal slumped to the ground.

I spun around. Cal lay crumpled on the floor beside me. I blinked. His eyes were shut. I couldn't see any blood. I looked up. Diamond was staring at me, his arm outstretched, a gun in his hand.

'Your mate just fainted,' Diamond snarled. 'I was aiming at the wall.'

I followed his gaze to a bullet hole in the wall by Cal's

head. Sunlight from the open door sent a ray of yellow across the dark corridor, highlighting the dent in the plaster.

Two men – clearly more bodyguards – raced up the corridor behind Diamond and the sunburnt guard. Diamond waved them back and they stopped. Each one carried a gun.

Trying to force away my rising panic, I weighed the situation up in my mind. I could teleport Cal, then turn and run outside, using telekinesis to slam the fire door shut. But I doubted very much if I'd be able to move fast enough to dodge all the weapons behind me.

I could get rid of the guns telekinetically, of course, but only one at a time. And even if I could take Diamond and the new guards by surprise, that would still leave the sunburnt guard I'd disarmed earlier. I knew from experience that once people had had their weapons torn out of their hands through telekinesis, they tended to hold on much tighter to them afterwards, even if they didn't understand exactly what had happened.

Diamond cocked his gun and levelled it at my face as the sunburnt guard – a wary look on his face – walked right round me and pulled the fire door shut. I was right; he was gripping his gun so hard his knuckles were white.

'How did you take my gun earlier?' he demanded.

'Quiet,' Diamond ordered 'I'm asking the questions. And the first answer I want is about McMurdo.'

My legs shook. With the fire doors shut, the corridor

was dark; light from the room we'd just run from sent spooky shadows along the wall. Diamond's earring glinted in the gloom.

'Talk,' he ordered. 'Why did McMurdo send you here if it wasn't to pay me?'

My panic rose further, whirling in my throat and up, inside my head. I couldn't think of a lie that would work. I couldn't think of anything to say except the truth.

'McMurdo sent us here to kill you,' I stammered. 'To get you alone and kill you.'

Diamond let out his breath as a low whistle. Then, to my surprise, he smiled.

'Kill me how exactly?' he said. 'Neither of you are armed. You're both kids.'

'What about what happened in the office, boss?' the guard protested. 'The gun I was holding . . . I think this boy somehow ripped it out of my hand.'

'Or you dropped it,' Diamond said with a sneer.

At my feet, Cal stirred. He let out a soft groan. Heart pounding, I stared back at Diamond.

'You're not going to take *my* gun,' he said. 'Or pull the trigger.'

'Actually, I am.' Not stopping to think, I teleported the gun out of his hand and balanced it in the air, turning it to face Diamond's head. He froze. The other guards started.

'Do it,' Cal whispered at my feet. 'Take the shot.'

I concentrated on the gun. I knew I only had seconds before the guards rushed me or before Diamond ordered them to shoot me. Just a few precious moments when everyone was too startled to move or speak.

I focused my attention on the trigger. The gun was already cocked. I'd seen how revolvers like this worked. I just had to pull the trigger back using telekinesis and the gun would fire into Diamond's temple.

Take the shot.

Take the shot.

The next second seemed to last an eternity and then I faced what I'd known all along.

I couldn't kill him. Certainly not like this, in cold blood.

It wasn't in me.

I let the gun fall to the ground.

As I looked down, someone hit me on the back of the head. The last thing I saw before I fell to the floor were Cal's trainers, rushing up to meet me.

20: Russian Roulette

My head hurt where the guard had hit me and my arm, bent beneath my body, was numb from where I'd been lying on it.

The floor under me was cold and hard. I groaned and opened my eyes. Cal's face filled my field of vision, his grey eyes peering anxiously down at me.

'Nico?' His face was very pale. 'Are you all right?'

I sat up, rubbing my head. 'I think so.' I looked around. We were inside some sort of concrete cellar. A row of barrels stood against one wall, some dusty bottles in a rack opposite. There was no window.

The recent events in the corridor and my inability to shoot Diamond suddenly rushed into my head. 'How long have I been out?' I asked.

'Only about ten minutes,' Cal said. He nodded towards the door. 'There are two guards out there, both armed and . . . and . . .' He hesitated.

'What?' I said.

'I told Diamond about the Medusa gene,' Cal blurted out. 'I'm sorry, but he kept pushing and pushing me about how you'd done that thing with his gun . . . you know, just holding it in mid-air. I felt so weird after fainting before and when he asked about me I . . . I showed him how I can move off the ground.' He sighed. 'I just wanted to pick you up and fly out of here, but there weren't any exits and everywhere I looked there was some guy with a gun and—'

'Don't sweat it,' I said. 'In case you didn't notice, I couldn't pull the trigger on Diamond so I'm not exactly finding a way out of this myself.'

'I'm glad you didn't shoot him,' Cal said firmly. 'Things like that change who you are . . .'

He looked down at the dusty concrete floor. I got the strong sense there was something he wasn't telling me.

'What's up?' I said.

Cal shook his head. A beat passed, but he said nothing.

'Okay, well, we have to get out of here,' I said, scrambling to my feet. A wave of nausea swelled inside me as I stood up. I clutched the back of my head again and leaned back against the wall.

'Are you all right?'

I nodded, looking around the room. I could easily teleport one of the barrels. Perhaps if I positioned it by the door, I could hurl it against the first guard who came in here . . . give us a chance to get away . . .

'Ed contacted me while you were unconscious,' Cal said. 'I told him where we were. He and Ketty are back at

Dad's. Sounds like they've all been going insane worrying about us . . .' He paused. 'Trouble is, they don't know exactly where Dylan is yet – and they can't risk calling the police until they know she's safe. They're on their way now, but Dad says it will take over an hour to get here by car. Diamond could come for us at any minute.'

'Right.' I teleported one of the barrels across the room and positioned it beside the door. 'I can use this to attack them,' I said. 'We'll make a run for it when they get here.'

Cal nodded. We stood in silence for a few moments. I thought back to my earlier suspicions about Cal and Avery being in league with McMurdo. They seemed ludicrous now.

'I guess Avery's, like, quite a cool dad, isn't he?' I said.

Cal shrugged. 'He's okay. Strict, though . . .' He paused. 'What about your . . . the guy you mentioned. Fred, is it?'

'Fergus?' I said. 'Well, Fergus is my stepdad. I don't know my real dad.' My thoughts went back to the DNA test results I'd heard Avery talking about on the phone. McMurdo hadn't given any indication there was any possibility that he knew about the test, let alone that I could be his son.

Cal's face reddened. 'You do know your real dad actually,' he said.

I stared at him. 'What d'you mean?'

A long pause. Cal met my eyes.

'It's Avery,' he said. 'He's your real dad.'

'*What?*' My head spun.

There was another long pause, then Cal sighed.

'When Avery started hacking into the files about the four of you in England, one of the things he checked out was your birth dates. I guess he realised that he could be your dad then. I overheard him talking about doing a DNA test off some drink you would have when you arrived, so I knew before I came to meet you that he suspected you were his son.'

So Avery *had* tested my DNA from the saliva on my lemonade glass. Well, that explained why Cal had been so hostile right from the start: Avery was his father and I could understand why he might not want to share him with a complete stranger.

I stood, letting the news sink in. Avery Jones was my dad. *That's* why he'd used the phrase: *Nico doesn't suspect a thing*. He'd been talking about my parentage, not some kind of double-cross deal with Rod McMurdo.

Before I could process this any further, the door banged open. Three of Diamond's men appeared, each one holding two guns, arms outstretched.

I glanced at the barrel I'd been planning on teleporting at them. Too late. I'd missed my chance. Now there were too many of them for me to deal with in one go.

The sunburnt guard from before was across the room before I could move. He grabbed my arm and yanked me towards the door.

'Come on,' he ordered. 'Both of you.'

We stumbled out of the cellar and up a short flight of

stairs, back to Diamond's office. This time the overhead light in the middle of the room was switched off though a table and two chairs had been set underneath it.

The surrounding sofas and chairs were filled with people – at least ten, I thought, as I glanced round. All men, smartly dressed and with drinks in their hands. They stared at me and Cal curiously. No one spoke.

The sunburnt guard shoved me into one of the seats at the small table in the centre of the room. Cal was pushed into the seat opposite. Diamond strode over, his fingers weighed down with heavy rings.

'Time for some entertainment,' he said with a smirk.

I glanced around the room. There were at least five guards in here standing at various points around the walls. Each one carried two guns, all of which were aimed at either my head, or Cal's.

My heart sank. No way could my telekinesis handle all those weapons at once.

'As you all know, I'm a huge fan of games of chance,' Diamond went on. He was, clearly, thoroughly enjoying himself. 'And games of chance are best when there's a lot at stake.'

What on earth did that mean?

Diamond held up his gun. 'There's one bullet in here,' he said. 'Which means Russian roulette.'

An excited murmur rippled round the room. I stared at him in confusion. I'd heard of Russian roulette, but I couldn't remember exactly what it was.

'Of course this will be no ordinary game.' Diamond held out the gun in his palm towards me. 'Nico, please use your telekinesis to take this . . . and point it at your head.'

I stared at him, shocked. I couldn't do it. I *wouldn't* do it.

'Get the gun into position,' Diamond repeated impatiently. 'Do it or I'll shoot you anyway.'

Heart pounding loudly, I teleported the gun into the air so that the barrel was pointing at my head. There was an audible gasp from the men in the room. Most of them leaned forward, trying to work out if it was some kind of trick.

'Bets, please,' Diamond cried. He threw me a nasty grin. Clearly, after my inability to shoot him earlier, he had no fears that I was about to turn the gun on him.

Excited chatter broke out all around us. The guard with narrow, mean eyes went round the room, taking everyone's bets.

My whole body trembled, but I kept the gun steady in the air.

A couple of men strode over, feeling the air between my head and the gun and the area around the gun, clearly trying to work out if it was suspended in the air with wires.

I kept my eyes on Cal, sitting opposite me. He looked petrified. I hadn't had time to think about it before, but it now occurred to me that if I was Avery's son, then he and his other children, including Cal, were my *family*.

Man, if *I* didn't die here, my *brother* would.

The seconds ticked by. A panicked jumble of thoughts

flashed in and out of my head. I thought of Avery and the others on their way to find us, I thought of Dylan trapped in McMurdo's room and I thought of Fergus back in England, hoping I was safe.

Most of all I thought of Ketty – her pretty, open face smiling at me. Being her boyfriend was the best thing in my life. I couldn't bear to leave her.

Part of me wanted to cry, but another part was numb, almost standing outside myself and watching what was happening.

There was no way my telekinesis was powerful enough to alter the course of a bullet, especially at such close range. Which left me with two choices.

One: I didn't shoot – or I turned the gun away from me and aimed a shot elsewhere. If I did this, Diamond had made it clear I'd be killed for disobeying him, whether the gun fired its single bullet or not.

Two: I shot at myself as Diamond had ordered – which would mean I had a one in six chance of dying. Six chambers, one bullet. The odds weren't great.

I forced myself to work it through. Three possible outcomes: be killed, shoot myself, or survive. And only one of those would result in me living beyond the next minute.

As the clamour in the room died down and all eyes turned expectantly to me, I knew that there was no choice. I swallowed.

'Take aim,' Diamond said.

I gritted my teeth, steadying the gun in the air beside me. I took a deep breath.

Don't think about it . . . don't think about it . . .

I fixed my eyes on Cal. If I was going to die, then at least the last thing I saw would be familiar.

I could just see the gun out of the corner of my eye. It was hovering beside my temple. I telekinetically squeezed down the trigger. I could see it shift, just slightly.

I held my breath and stared at Cal, shutting out the rest of the room.

Then I closed my eyes and pulled the trigger.

21: The Getaway

At the last minute I turned the gun and fired into the ceiling. The gun clicked – an empty, hollow sound that meant the single bullet wasn't in the chamber that had fired.

I opened my eyes with a huge sigh of relief. Cal was still sitting right in front of me, his face frozen in panic.

"You cheated," Diamond roared.

Around us, the room erupted. I laid the gun on the table. For a second, wild elation surged through me, then it was like my body crumbled on the inside, collapsing in on itself. I wanted to bawl my eyes out, but instead I turned to Diamond.

'I still pulled the trigger,' I said, my voice harsh and steady. 'Now let us go.'

Diamond shook his head. He pointed at Cal. 'Shoot at him.'

'*What?*'

He couldn't be serious. My mouth fell open. 'No *way*.'

Diamond bent down so his mouth was right by my ear.

'They want to see you fire the gun without touching it and I want to see you do it without cheating,' he hissed. 'Do it or I'll kill him anyway.'

He shoved the gun towards me on the table.

Heart pounding, I teleported it into the air. As I moved it towards Cal, the room fell silent again. Hushed awe and anticipation filled the air.

I placed the gun in position against Cal's head. I'd avoided looking at his face before. Now I shifted my focus to take him in. His eyes were wide and terrified.

This was unbearable.

'I can't,' I said. 'He's my brother.'

Diamond laughed. 'C'mon, sport,' he said. 'You don't look anything alike.'

I glanced back at Cal. It was true: his skin was fairer than mine and his hair was white-blond while mine was dark.

'Okay, he's my half-brother,' I insisted.

'You're making it up.' The smile slid from Diamond's face. 'Get on with it. Everyone's watching. Pull the trigger.'

I focused on the gun again, unable to bear the terror in Cal's eyes. I forced myself to think through the options again. The possible outcomes were the same as before except shooting at Cal was taking a risk with *his* life. Not *mine*.

In that moment I knew I couldn't do it. Whatever happened, there was no way I could shoot him.

I couldn't shoot Cal. I couldn't shoot anybody.

An idea sprang into my head. There was no time to think it through, I just had to hope that I could carry it off . . . and that Cal wasn't too traumatised to help me.

In a single movement I teleported the gun into my hand and lunged at Diamond. He stumbled and I pushed him against the table, pressing the barrel of the gun against his neck.

Shocked cries in the room. The guards all around stared uncertainly at Diamond.

'Grab him,' Diamond hissed quietly at the guard standing immediately behind him. 'There aren't any bullets in the gun. *Grab* him.'

No bullets? So the whole Russian roulette game had been a trick. Furious, I raised my hand and focused on teleporting the guard at the door. Taken by complete surprise, the man rose off his feet, into the air. He let out a terrified yell. The crowd around us shrank back as I shoved the man through the air, teleporting him forcefully to the floor. He landed heavily. For a second, everyone stared at him, totally freaked out.

I glanced at Cal. 'Move us,' I commanded.

He blinked, taking a moment to understand me.

'NOW!' I yelled.

In a flash, Cal was in the air. He reached for me . . . grabbed me . . . We flew to the door, terrified gasps all around us.

'Get them!' Diamond shouted.

But we were at the door. I opened it telekinetically and

Cal hauled us through and along the corridor. I turned, trying to keep my body as still as possible as Cal negotiated the dark, narrow pathway, and slammed the door shut behind us. I twisted my hand to lock it.

Immediately, a shot fired.

Cal stiffened beside me.

'They're shooting at the lock,' I said. 'Hurry!'

We flew faster . . . up the stairs . . . along the corridor. I flung open doors as we passed them. *There*. A storeroom cluttered with cleaning things – with a window big enough for us to get through. I flung the window open and Cal flew us through. Once outside, he hovered in the air, clutching at my arm to steady me.

I looked around. We were in a deserted side street. It was dark. There was no sign of McMurdo.

'Where now?' Cal asked in a terrified voice.

'Up high!' I ordered.

In a flash Cal had zoomed into the air, high, high above the streets below. I looked down. Big mistake. I lost my grip on his arm and slipped. As I slid, I just managed to grab hold of his ankle. My fingers dug into his leg.

Cal looked down at me, his eyes wide. 'Hold on!'

We soared above the buildings. This time it wasn't so hard to keep my legs and arms together which, I could feel, helped us move faster. I looked down. A tall block a few hundred metres away had a square, flat roof.

'Let's land there.' I pointed at the rooftop.

Cal nodded. He dived towards the rooftop, stopping

suddenly to hover a few metres above it. I was jerked backwards by the motion.

'Sorry,' Cal murmured as he lowered us to land gently. 'I'm kind of jittery.'

As I touched the concrete ground, my legs started shaking. I sank down, unable to stand for another second. As the tension flooded out of me, what Cal had said struck me as the funniest thing I'd ever heard. 'Jittery,' I repeated, starting to laugh. 'Jittery.' I put my head in my hands, giggling helplessly.

Cal stood over me, panting from the exertion of flying. I glanced up at him, tears of laughter now leaking out of my eyes.

'Man, if you are jittery, I'm a freakin' wreck.'

Cal stared down at me, his expression furious for a second. Then he, too, sank to the ground and doubled over with laughter.

We couldn't stop for at least a minute. Every time one of us tried to straighten out, the other set both of us off again. But at last the laughter dried up and we stared at each other.

I shook my head, realising just how wrong my first impression of Cal had been. Cal himself lay back on the ground.

'Where now?' he asked.

'We have to find the house where McMurdo was holding us earlier. Dylan's still there – and once McMurdo realises we've double-crossed him, he'll kill her. We have to get to her first.'

Cal nodded. He sat up and looked across the lights of the city. 'I think McMurdo's house was over there,' he said, pointing eastwards.

'Let's head that way, then,' I said.

As we stood up, Cal punched me lightly in the shoulder.

'Thanks for saving me back there, er . . . bro,' he said. 'For a moment, I thought you were really gonna shoot me.'

I grinned. 'No worries,' I said. 'Ketty would have killed me if I hadn't done the right thing.'

Cal's face reddened. He looked away.

Why had I mentioned Ketty's name? I'd completely forgotten how, just hours before, I'd been insanely jealous of the way Cal had been all over her. He still wasn't looking at me. Man, maybe he really did like her. Maybe she really liked him. I shook myself. I couldn't let thoughts of Ketty distract me now.

'Come on, man,' I said, forcing a note of steel into my voice. 'Let's go.'

We soared into the air again, flying high above the houses and buildings, heading east. As we flew, Ed appeared in my mind.

Nico, are you all right?

I quickly communicated everything that had happened. *We're looking for McMurdo's house now*, I thought-spoke. *We have to get Dylan.*

I know, Ed thought-spoke back. A few minutes later, Ed contacted me again with McMurdo's address, which he'd found using Clusterchaos.

'I know the area,' Cal said when I told him. 'Yeah, that fits . . . that's where we were this arvo.'

Meet you there, I thought-spoke to Ed.

Okay. Ed hesitated. *Avery says to wait outside for us when you get there.*

Sure.

Cal flew with amazing speed, far faster than when he'd brought the four of us to Sydney earlier. He explained it was easier to move with just one other person, rather than having to extend his energy to four others. That made sense to me – it was kind of like being able to lift lighter items using my telekinesis, but struggling to move something really heavy. He kept high above the buildings for most of the journey. It wasn't a highly populated area – we just had to hope that anyone who *did* catch sight of us wouldn't be able to work out exactly what they were seeing. At least it was dark.

I didn't want to think about what Diamond and his men would make of my telekinesis. Keeping our powers secret had always been a priority and now I'd used my ability in front of an entire roomful of people. As had Cal.

We reached McMurdo's house within a few minutes. From high in the sky, using the street lamps to see by, I scanned the area for signs that he was there.

'His van's not here,' Cal said. 'He's probably still outside Diamond's bar, waiting for us.'

I nodded, my heart pounding. A moment later we'd landed a few metres from the house in the shelter of a copse of trees.

I took a second to study the door we'd left the house through earlier. It looked like a fairly straightforward lock to open.

'Suppose McMurdo's releasing the Medutox into the whole house?' Cal said. 'We won't be able to use our powers.'

'It won't matter if I can open the door from here,' I said. 'We'll move as soon as Avery arr—'

'Help!' A high-pitched shout sounded faintly from inside the house. 'Help!'

I froze. *Dylan*. Cal and I exchanged looks.

'Are you thinking what I'm thinking?' Cal said slowly.

I nodded. 'We can't wait,' I said. 'Let's get inside now.'

And, side by side, we rushed towards the house.

22: The Proof

I reached out my hands as we ran, then jerked my wrist to the side, focusing on the lock inside the door.

I felt the lock release. *Yes.* I sped up, Cal at my heels.

'Wait out here,' I panted as we reached the door. 'That way you won't lose your Medusa ability. I'll go in and get Dylan. You can fly us both out of here in a minute.'

Cal hesitated a moment, then nodded. 'Okay,' he said. 'Yell if you need me.'

I darted inside, then stopped to get my bearings. I remembered this shadowy hallway from earlier. The room where Dylan was, presumably, still being held was two doors down on the right. As I crept towards it, I listened out for noise from the rest of the house. The place was silent.

I hurried towards Dylan's door, unlocking it with another twist of my hand. At least my telekinesis was intact. I reached the door and pushed it open as Dylan must have pulled it from the inside. I stumbled towards her.

'Nico!' she gasped.

'Are you okay?' I whispered, peering into the corridor again to check no one else was here. 'We heard you yelling.'

'Yeah, I was trying to break the door down.' Dylan grimaced, rubbing her shoulder. 'It was too heavy, especially without my Medusa power.' She stepped outside the room and shut the door. 'McMurdo's got that Medutox stuff on slow release into the room, but it's not in the rest of the house.' She paused. 'Where is McMurdo anyway?'

'We gave him the slip. Cal's outside. Let's go.'

'Wait.' Dylan grabbed my arm. 'What about McMurdo's evidence on Geri? He said it was here, remember? It's probably in his safe upstairs. You could open it, like you opened the vault in the bank.'

I stared at her. 'How d'you even know he's *got* a safe upstairs?'

'McMurdo mentioned it.' She gripped my arm more tightly. 'Come *on*, Nico. McMurdo's not here and—'

'He could be back any minute,' I said.

'But the film of Geri's confession is proof that she killed my mom and dad,' Dylan insisted, her eyes wide. 'If we have that, we can discredit her claim that we killed Bookman.'

She was right. The evidence on Geri was the only thing that was going to get us home to England.

'Where exactly is this safe?' I said.

Dylan flashed me a grin and raced towards the stairs in the corner of the hallway. I followed her up, two steps at a time.

'How long after you'd been sprayed with Medutox did it take for your Medusa power to come back?' Dylan asked.

'About half an hour.'

Dylan groaned. 'That's ages. I hate being without it.' She pointed to the door opposite the head of the stairs. 'The safe is through there.'

We ran into the room ahead and switched on the light. It was large and neat and ordered – cupboards down one side, a table and work lamp with a laptop surrounded by piles of paper on the other. The overall effect was smart, though not particularly expensive. Nowhere near in the same league as Avery's ranch. A large painting hung on the wall beside the desk. A quick glance around suggested the area it concealed was the most likely place for the safe.

'Help me with this,' I said.

Seconds later the painting was off the wall and Dylan and I were staring at the built-in safe.

'I don't think we'll be able to pull this one out,' she murmured.

I made a face, remembering how the two of us had ripped out the safe in Fergus's Edinburgh house. Back there, the plaster wall had been crumbling away and the safe was old. Here, the steel shone like someone had recently polished it and the whole thing was set firmly into its surroundings with rivets.

'Like you said, opening this can't be any harder than feeling my way round the bolts in that bank vault; it's just a case of not rushing it.'

187

Dylan rolled her eyes. 'Awesome,' she snarled. 'Because we have all the time in the world.'

Ignoring her, I held my hands over the safe and moved the knob telekinetically round. I closed my eyes, all my energy focused on waiting for the ridge that the internal workings would hit when I'd reached the first number in the combination.

There.

I opened my eyes. Dylan had wandered across the room to the window and was peering out at the street below.

I squeezed my eyes tight shut again and felt for the next number. It came up quickly, but the third number took ages to find. I had to rotate the external knob several times before I felt the ridge and stopped.

As I searched for the fourth number, I could sense Dylan pacing the room, her impatience filling the air. I tried to block her presence out, concentrating on the work in front of me.

At last the safe clicked open. Dylan was beside me in seconds, pulling open the door. She reached in, foraging through a pile of notebooks and papers.

'Here!' She held up an old-style CD in a plastic case that was at the bottom of the pile. It was unmarked.

'Let's try it.' I took the CD and turned on the MacBook at the desk across the room. It hummed speedily into life. I found the disk drive and inserted the CD.

We stood in front of the screen, watching as the DVD player program flashed up.

'Come on, come on,' Dylan muttered.

I held my breath as the screen fizzled into a grainy recording of what looked like another room in McMurdo's house. A print very similar to the one concealing the safe hung on the wall. Geri stood beside it, visible from the waist up. She was speaking as the film started, her voice full of emotion. It took me a couple of sentences to catch on to what she was saying.

'*I had to kill William,*' she said. '*It was the only way to protect the Medusa Project. Now you've got to keep your end of the bargain.*'

'That's it,' Dylan said, clasping her hands together. As she spoke, a door slammed downstairs.

'McMurdo!' Dylan reached for the keyboard, holding her finger over the eject button.

As she clicked down, footsteps echoed up from down-stairs. It sounded like more than one person. I crept to the door, my heart beating fast. As I did so, Ed chose that moment to contact me telepathically.

Nico, any sign of McMur—?

Ed, listen, he's in the house and he's not alone. I need to focus.

Ed vanished without another word.

I stood in the doorway. The low murmur of voices drifted up the stairs.

I crept back to Dylan. She was still standing over the Mac, prodding frantically at the keys.

'They don't know we're up here yet,' I whispered. 'Let's go.'

189

'I can't get the freakin' disk out,' she hissed. 'It's really old and this is a modern computer.'

'What?' I pressed the eject button myself. The computer didn't even register the motion. I swore under my breath.

'What are we going to do?' Dylan said desperately.

'Take the whole laptop.' I slapped the lid shut.

'She's gone!' McMurdo's cry roared up the stairs towards us.

'Hurry!' Dylan grabbed the Mac off the desk.

We raced to the window as the sound of footsteps echoed up the stairs.

I opened the window, my heart in my mouth. I looked out. Where was Cal? He must have been hiding close by because he seemed to zoom out of nowhere.

He hovered outside the window. 'What are you guys doing?' he hissed. 'McMurdo's just gone into the house. He's—'

'Help us through.' Dylan passed him the computer and clambered onto the ledge.

'Be careful.' Cal held the Mac precariously under one arm and reached for Dylan's wrist with his free hand.

Outside, on the landing, the footsteps pounded closer.

Holding her steady, Cal helped Dylan to slide off the ledge until she was hovering beside him in mid-air, gripping his shoulder. Cal held out his hand to me. 'Come on.'

Behind me the door opened. A shot fired, whizzing past my ear.

Cal vanished. I spun round, raising the desk beside me off the floor. I hurled it at the figure in the doorway. It crashed in front of her: Geri Paterson.

We stared at each other. Geri's eyes were round with shock. My first thought – more of a desperate hope, really – was that maybe this wasn't Geri at all, but Amy. I searched for the giveaway signs Amy had displayed when she'd taken on Geri's appearance. But the woman in front of me in her smart red suit and sleek blonde bob had all the poise and confidence I knew from the real Geri and none of the round-shouldered meekness of Amy's imitation version.

'What the hell are you doing, Nico?' Geri snapped. 'What have you done with Dylan?'

I forced myself not to look through the window to where I hoped Cal and Dylan were now safe. Instead, I focused on the picture, still propped up by the wall. If I could slam that against Geri, I could maybe run past her and get out through the front door downstairs.

As I raised the painting telekinetically into the air, McMurdo rushed into the room. He stood, panting, beside Geri, his spray can in his hand.

'For goodness' sake, use the Medutox!' Geri shrieked.

As I hurled the painting towards them, McMurdo dodged sideways. The Medutox spray hit me in the face. I tried not to breathe in, but it was no good. I could feel it burning the back of my throat. Desperate now, I turned round, hands outstretched, searching for another object to throw at them.

My eyes lit on the floor lamp in the corner. I tried to lift it up, but the Medutox had already taken effect. My telekinesis was gone.

Heart racing, I glanced at the window. I could see Cal out of the corner of my eye. He was alone – presumably having deposited Dylan safely on the ground – where Geri and McMurdo couldn't see him. Man, if I could just reach the window, Cal would help me get away.

But McMurdo must have followed my gaze. As I took my first step towards Cal, McMurdo rushed over to the window himself. He pointed his Medutox can at Cal and pressed the nozzle.

'No!' I yelled, as the fine mist sprayed out.

Cal somersaulted backwards through the air and out of my range of vision. I ran to the window. Had the Medutox reached him? No.

Overwhelmed with relief, I watched Cal landing in the trees beside a waiting Dylan. They disappeared from view.

I turned back to Geri. She was looking at me, a gun in her elegantly manicured hand. She narrowed her eyes as she took in the open safe and the upturned desk.

'They've got the proof,' she said furiously, turning her gun from me to McMurdo. 'They've got the evidence against me.'

McMurdo stared at the gun. I suddenly registered that he was as much Geri's prisoner as I was. And, from the way he was looking at her revolver, I guessed that, like me, he was working out his chances of getting it away from her.

'Cal will take the evidence to his father,' McMurdo said. 'And Avery Jones will know how to get it to Interpol.' He shot Geri a wry smile. 'Even you can't control Interpol, Geri.'

My heart thudded. At the mention of Avery's name, I remembered that he and the others were on their way here. When Ed had made contact before, he'd said they would only be a few minutes. Maybe I didn't have to hold on much longer.

'Then we'll get to Avery Jones before he has a chance to contact the police,' Geri said. 'Between the three of us we should be able to get the evidence back before Avery can show it to anyone.'

'Okay,' McMurdo said, eyeing Geri's gun again.

'I'm not helping you,' I said defiantly. 'There's nothing you can do to me that will make me go after that evidence for you.'

'Really?' Geri said with a cold smile. 'Maybe not to *you* . . . but perhaps you'll help me if someone else's life is at stake.'

'Who?' I said. What was she talking about? None of the others were here.

Geri took a step sideways, then dragged a girl into view. She was bound and gagged, her head bowed.

As she looked up, I realised with a jolt that it was Ketty.

23: Protecting Ketty

My head spun. What was Ketty doing here? How had Geri managed to find her?

She stood looking towards the floor, the ropes round her wrists digging into her skin. Her eyes above the gag were wild with fear. I'd never seen Ketty look so completely terrified.

I clenched my fists, then released them, instinctively trying to engage my telekinesis to undo her bindings. It was a moment before I remembered the Medutox I'd just been sprayed with.

I was helpless.

'Why've you taken Ketty?' I yelled.

Geri shook her head. She beckoned McMurdo over. Holding the gun primed in front of her, Geri spoke to him under her breath. I couldn't hear what she said. I turned back to Ketty who was still standing in the doorway, her body shaking, her eyes fixed on me.

I couldn't work it out. I'd only been communicating

with Ed a few minutes ago. Why hadn't he mentioned Ketty was missing? My mind raced on, desperate to work it out. Either Geri had somehow captured them *all*, which wasn't conceivable in the time that had elapsed, or Ketty hadn't been with Ed and Avery when Ed made contact with me. Which meant *they* didn't know Geri had her.

It suddenly hit me that there was no way I could warn Ed about any of this. Even if he tried to make contact, I wouldn't be able to hear him because of the Medutox.

'Come on!' Geri's sharp voice brought me back to the present.

As she bound my wrists, McMurdo led Ketty downstairs.

Keeping one eye on Geri's gun, I followed them to the ground floor.

As we left the house, I looked around for Cal and Dylan. No sign. Surely they were watching us, though? And surely Avery and Ed couldn't be far away?

McMurdo led Ketty down the yard and bundled her into the back seat of a large station wagon parked outside the house.

Geri indicated I should get in next to Ketty. She herself sat in the passenger seat at the front, while McMurdo slid into the driver's position and switched on the engine. I gave a last look around. There was no sign of any of the others.

'Get in,' Geri snapped. 'Hurry.'

As I got in, she slid shut the partition that separated the front from the back of the car.

She turned to McMurdo, presumably giving him an order about where to drive. As we set off, Geri took out her BlackBerry and started prodding at the keys. I was too far away to see what exactly she was doing.

Again, I tried to use my telekinesis. The rope round my wrists, which would have been so simple to untie under normal circumstances, was completely impossible for me to undo.

It was unbelievably frustrating. I sat back with a sigh and turned to Ketty. She was still looking at me, her golden-brown eyes wide with alarm.

Keeping an eye on Geri up front, I shuffled across the back seat so I was closer to Ketty. There was no way I could undo the ropes on our wrists or the gag in Ketty's mouth, but I could talk and she could listen.

I leaned my head close in to Ketty's ear. She stiffened.

'We're going to be all right,' I whispered. 'Cal and Dylan were outside the house. They must have seen us come out – they'll be able to follow us. How did you get separated from Ed and Avery?'

Ketty shook her head, presumably to indicate the impossibility of answering.

'Sorry.' I swallowed. 'Listen,' I said. 'I just found out Avery's my dad and Cal's my brother. That's why Cal was kind of weird with me earlier. I . . . I . . . know I overreacted when you went off with him.' I hesitated. 'But he's cool.'

Ketty drew her head back, gazing at me with soft, curious eyes.

As she looked at me, I suddenly imagined just how awful it would be if she decided she preferred being with Cal to me.

My heart skipped a beat and I realised I had no idea what to say to make her stay. Girls liked to hear about your feelings . . . that much I knew . . .

I took a deep breath and leaned closer to her ear again.

'I haven't said this for ages, but . . .'

I stammered to a halt and glanced to the front of the car. Geri was still bent over her BlackBerry while McMurdo was concentrating on the fast, empty road ahead of us. It was almost dawn. There were fields all around. Mountains in the distance. My heart hammered. Ketty raised her eyebrows, waiting for me to finish my sentence.

'I love you,' I whispered. 'And I won't let anyone hurt you.'

Tears welled in her eyes. I looked away, staring out of the window, my cheeks burning. I'd only said those words once before – just before Fox Academy got blown up. It felt like years had passed since then.

Half an hour later, McMurdo turned the car onto a dirt track. Brown dust swirled in the air behind us. Another few minutes and I recognised the approach to Avery's ranch.

McMurdo stopped at the end of the drive. The swimming

pool glittered in the distance, the low sun glancing off its glassy surface.

Geri ordered us out of the car.

I stood next to Ketty, watching for any movement. Would Philly or Caro or any of the little kids be there? Part of me wanted someone to see us and raise the alarm. Another part of me hoped that they were all safely out of the house. As I thought this, it struck me that all those little kids were my brothers and sisters, too, just like Cal. I had this enormous family I didn't even know.

'Avery's on his way here,' Geri said. 'I've told him if he turns up with any kind of outside support, I'll kill you.' She narrowed her eyes and tilted her head to one side. 'He seems *most* concerned about you, Nico. But then that's to be expected, I suppose, given what he's just found out about your relationship.'

I stared back at her. 'How long have *you* known?'

'That Avery was your father? He just told me.' Geri laughed that tinkly little laugh of hers. 'Goodness, I had no idea before. Your mother told no one. Anyway, it's all working to my advantage. Avery's absolutely frantic about you.'

'Why are you doing this?' I said. 'Why don't you just accept that it's time the truth came out . . . that you have to pay for killing Dylan's parents and that agent, Bookman?'

Geri shook her head. 'There's no need to keep raking up all that. I already told Dylan. Her father was impossible

to deal with and her mother just knew too much . . . Bookman deserved to die, manipulative old blackmailer . . .'

I glanced at McMurdo. He was standing, watching us.
Again, I got the strong sense he was waiting for Geri to
miss a step so he could go for her gun. I shivered. I wasn't
sure I'd be any safer if he was in control of what happened
next than Geri.

'You let me down, Nico,' McMurdo said slowly. 'I
sent you to kill Diamond. You're going to pay for
failing.'

'And how are you going to make me?' I snapped. 'You're
just as much Geri's prisoner as me and Ketty.'

'Ketty?' McMurdo sneered. 'I don't—'

'Shut up.' Geri turned on him.

She held out the gun. McMurdo reluctantly put his hands
in the air.

'This is what's going to happen,' Geri said. 'Avery will
be here soon with the evidence against me. I'm going to
take the evidence and drive away. End of story. I won't
come after you. You won't come after me.'

I shook my head. 'But that won't clear our names,' I
argued. 'The police in England will still think we killed
Bookman. We won't be able to go home.'

'Then stay here with Avery Jones,' Geri snapped. 'He's
your father, after all.'

'What about Fergus?' I said. 'He's my dad, too. And
England's my home . . . not just for me, but for Ed and
Ketty, too.'

'You'll just have to move on,' Geri said briskly. 'Let go.'

I opened my mouth to say that I'd never let go when it came to bringing Geri to justice. But before I could speak, McMurdo lunged for Geri's gun.

I jumped as the shot rang out, loud and echoey across the fields. I stared, my eyeballs feeling like they would burst out of my head, as McMurdo flew backwards, clutching his stomach.

He slumped to the dusty ground. A trickle of blood seeped out from under his body. The world seemed to stand still.

Ketty shuffled closer to me. I leaned my shoulder against hers. It was the only way I could think of to show her I was here for her.

McMurdo's face was pressed against the ground. He wasn't moving.

Geri marched over to him, briskly feeling for his pulse. I realised I was holding my breath and took in a lungful of crisp, dawn air.

'He's not going to make it,' she said, straightening up.

I shivered. I'd known she was a murderer, but it was completely different to see someone killed. I looked away from McMurdo's body, sick to my stomach.

In the distance I could just make out a car turning off the main road. That had to be Avery. Geri had seen it, too. 'We're going inside,' she said, grabbing Ketty by the arm. 'Avery will meet us there.'

As I stumbled beside them towards the house, Geri spoke again.

'My gun is pointing at Ketty's head, Nico,' she said coldly. 'If you do anything against me, I *will* kill her. Understand?'

I had no choice but to agree.

24: Upload

We walked around the ranch in silence. Geri had untied Ketty's feet, but her hands and mouth were still bound. I couldn't put my arm round her because my own wrists were tied, but I walked as close to her as possible.

Ketty glanced at me as we reached the swimming pool. Geri was already at the side door to the ranch house. To my surprise it was open.

'Avery's called his wife,' Geri said. 'Told her to leave the door unlocked for us before she and the maid left with the kids. He says you're to take us somewhere called the Snug – where's that?'

'Down here.' I led the way along the corridor and into the open-plan living area. At least now I knew that Philly and Caro and the little kids would be safe.

Geri settled herself down on the couch where Avery had sat during our first meeting. I turned to look out of the window. The sun was getting higher in the sky. As I watched, Avery's car reached Geri's and slowed down.

I could just make out Avery's face turned to the open window beside him. He must be able to see McMurdo's body from there.

All of a sudden the car sped up again. Avery drove rapidly up the drive, then raced out of the car, a briefcase in his hand. He ran past the porch and out of sight. I peered at the car. The closed windows were dark. Was Ed in there? What about Dylan or Cal?

I was sure they would have had plenty of time to reach Avery, but had Avery brought them here?

I turned around. Geri was pushing Ketty into one of the Snug's many chairs. She drew out a pair of handcuffs and fastened Ketty to the arm of the chair, then bent over and whispered something in her ear.

'What are you saying?' I demanded.

'Quiet,' Geri snapped, straightening up and taking out her gun.

Footsteps in the corridor outside. Geri and I turned towards the door as Avery burst through it. He stared around the room, speedily taking in the whole scene. His eyes widened as he caught sight of Ketty.

'How did you get hold of *her*?' he said.

I gulped. Clearly, Avery hadn't known that Geri had kidnapped Ketty. Did that mean he'd lost track of Ed, Cal and Dylan, too?

Geri said nothing in response, simply cocked her gun and held it against Ketty's head.

I met Ketty's gaze, trying to communicate that everything

was going to be all right. Ketty looked back at me, her expression above the gag around her mouth calmer than it had been earlier. She gave me a quick nod and my heart skipped a beat. What did that nod mean? Maybe she'd had a positive vision of the near future. It seemed unlikely – after all, Ketty tended to lose her Medusa ability when she was stressed. Still, I felt better believing that maybe she'd seen into the next few minutes and that her calm, confident nod was meant to reassure me.

'Are you all right, Nico?' Avery asked anxiously.

'I'm fine,' I said.

Avery turned to Geri and held up his briefcase. 'Here's the computer. Cal and Dylan brought it to me directly from McMurdo's house. The CD is still inside it. Now let Nico and Ketty go.'

'Not until I've seen the film on the CD,' Geri snapped.

Avery frowned. His hand shook as he laid the briefcase on the coffee table and drew out the Mac. He set it down. Keeping her gun trained on me, Geri strode towards him.

'Play the CD.'

Avery did as he was told. We watched the film I'd seen earlier. It was an absolute confession.

As Geri watched, a look of horror crept into her eyes.

'Did you make a copy of this?' she demanded. 'Has anyone else seen it?'

'Of course not,' Avery protested. 'Cal gave the laptop to me less than an hour ago and I've spent the entire time since bringing it here. Anyway, the CD is stuck. We can't get it out, so there's no way we could have copied it onto another CD or given it to someone else.'

'You could have stored it in a flash drive or emailed it somewhere,' Geri pointed out.

'Yes, but we haven't.' Avery's voice was strained. 'Geri, I don't want to do anything to upset this situation further. You have Ketty and . . . and my son.' He looked at me as he said the words. 'I don't care about *anything* except their safety.'

Geri stared at him, clearly trying to decide whether he was telling the truth. I tore my eyes away from Avery's anxious face and focused on a cushion on the sofa behind her. The effects of Medutox wore off after about thirty minutes. It had surely been that long since McMurdo had last sprayed me. I concentrated on trying to make the cushion move. A flicker of telekinetic energy pulsed through me, then disappeared. The edge of the cushion shifted a millimetre. It was something . . . but nowhere near enough.

Geri was now prodding at the keyboard, trying to eject the disk. After a moment, she stood back with an exasperated sigh.

'I'll take the computer,' she said. 'It's not as if McMurdo is going to need it again.'

'I saw what you did to him,' Avery said. He glanced at me. 'You can't possibly hope to get away with his murder.'

'It wasn't murder, it was self-defence,' Geri snapped. 'Just remember I'm letting you off lightly here, Avery. You

205

get to keep your family safe. All I ask in return is that you don't attempt to pursue me.'

I looked at the screen behind her. The video showing her confession was over. I focused on the mouse pad on the computer, putting all my effort into depressing it telekinetically. With a jerk, the cursor sped across the screen.

Yes. An idea flickered into my head. I glanced back at Geri. She was still looking at Avery.

'Why didn't you tell me Nico was my son,' Avery said bitterly. 'You'd met me in London. You knew where to find me.'

Keeping one ear on the conversation, I turned back to the screen.

'Goodness, your ego is bigger than William Fox's,' Geri said tartly. 'I *didn't* know until McMurdo told me earlier.'

I focused on the screen. Using my telekinesis, I moved the cursor to save the file containing the film of Geri's confession to the desktop, then looked for the internet browser on the machine.

'You *must* have known,' Avery insisted. 'William would have wanted to know the identity of the father before he implanted Lucia with the gene.'

It gave me a start to hear Avery say my mum's name. It suddenly occurred to me that if Avery was my dad, he must have had some sort of relationship with my mum. But there was no time to think about that now.

I shook myself and focused on the screen again. The internet browser was open now. I used telekinesis on the letter keys so that they spelled out the name of the site I was looking for . . . the site that was going to help us get our revenge on Geri, whether she took the computer or not.

I focused on the last letter of the URL I wanted and pressed 'go'.

The site flashed up.

www.youtube.com

I set to work.

25: Exposure

I entered my YouTube user name. I could feel my telekinesis getting stronger . . . I could manipulate all the
computer keys and the mouse pad with only the lightest
of efforts.

I glanced at Geri. She was still talking.

I just had to enter the title of my post: *UK govt agent
Geri Paterson admits to murd*—

'What are you doing?' Geri roared.

She raced towards the computer, her eyes wide.

Telekinetic energy surged through me. With a focused
effort, I released the rope that bound my wrists and leaped
forwards. But Avery had already moved, He reached Geri
as she turned.

The shot rang out – the scene a virtual repeat of
McMurdo's shooting. Avery flew backwards, clutching
his arm. Geri advanced on him, her gun gripped tightly
in her hand.

Avery slumped to the ground, his eyes shut. I stared in

horror, my mind tumbling over and over itself with the shock.

And then a muffled yell from Ketty brought me back to my senses.

I swivelled back to the computer. I could still upload the file at least.

'Stop!' Geri cried. 'Stop or I shoot her.'

I froze, then looked around. Geri was pacing towards Ketty, her gun tightly gripped in her hand. As she passed the computer, she slammed the lid down.

I swallowed. Geri's face was screwed up with an intense fury. I glanced back at Avery. He was lying, clearly unconscious, on the floor. A trail of blood was seeping out from underneath his arm.

'I warned you, Nico!' Geri shrieked. She reached Ketty and shoved the gun against her temple.

'No!' I cried.

I reached out, determined to wrench the gun telekinetically out of Geri's hands. But she was holding it too tightly.

'Get back!' Geri shouted. 'Stop!' She pressed the gun harder against Ketty's skin.

I stopped, the blood pounding in my ears.

Ketty stared back at me, her eyes huge and round and full of fear.

'Please.' The voice that came out of me was not one I recognised. I dropped to my knees. 'Please, Geri, don't hurt her.'

Geri's whole face tightened. 'You've blown it, Nico,'

she said. 'I realise that there's no alternative. And I can see how to play it, too . . . There was a showdown between Avery and McMurdo. You and Ketty got caught in the crossfire. I tried to stop the shooting, but the two men were beside themselves . . . wouldn't listen to reason . . .'

I listened to her words, but I couldn't take them in. My mind raced. There had to be a way of stopping Geri.

'No,' I said.

As I spoke, Ketty lunged forward in her chair, clearly aiming to knock Geri off balance. I leaped forwards, but before I could reach them, Geri had pushed Ketty away with such force that Ketty's chair toppled over backwards, Ketty still strapped inside it.

I gasped as the chair and Ketty crashed to the floor behind the low table.

Geri pointed her gun downwards, at where Ketty was lying. She kept her eyes on me. 'I won't make you watch me kill her,' she said coolly. 'That's something, isn't it?'

'Please, Geri?'

'Three,' she said.

No. I summoned all my focus. I was going to have to try teleporting the gun again.

'Two,' she said.

I put every atom of energy I could muster into the effort, but Geri was gripping it too tightly. The gun wouldn't budge.

'Please,' I sobbed.

Geri threw me a thin, cruel smile.

'One.'

'NO!' As I cried out, I heard the same word being yelled by other voices behind me.

Suddenly I felt a hand round my arm, lifting me off the ground. A quick flash of Geri's shocked face, and my arms and legs were flung out. Geri vanished into a blur as something . . . someone . . . hurled me round like a machete. I flexed my feet. A split second later my heels rammed into Geri's shoulder.

She flew backwards. Her gun fired into the ceiling. She landed on her back on the floor.

The hand holding me let me go. I fell to the ground, narrowly missing the edge of the couch by the door. I lay for a second feeling dizzy, gasping for breath, then scrambled to my feet.

Cal was standing next to me. It was he who'd flown into the room and, using the momentum created by that movement, hurled me across the room and into Geri. Dylan was here, too . . . and Ed by the door.

All three of them had their eyes fixed on Geri. She was on her feet again. Her hair, normally a sleek blonde helmet, was ruffled with flecks of powder from the ceiling plaster and her smart jacket was torn along the sleeve, but she held her gun steadily as she pointed to the computer on the table.

'Give me the Mac,' Geri ordered.

'No.' Dylan stepped right in front of her. 'Give me the gun.'

I turned. Across the room, Avery lay slumped, the blood

211

still seeping out of him. Further away, behind the low table, Ketty was still on the ground. I could just see her foot peeking out from behind the table.

A shot fired. I spun round. Geri had fired into Dylan, but Dylan was still standing.

A smile spread over Dylan's face. 'It's over, Geri.'

She reached out and grabbed Geri's gun, then turned it on Geri herself.

Geri blinked, her eyes suddenly sharper and wilder.

'You don't know how to use that,' she snapped.

'Actually, I do,' said Dylan.

For a second, I was torn in so many directions I stood paralysed. What I wanted to do most was rush over to Ketty, but Avery needed my help more.

I tugged at Cal's arm. 'Avery was shot in the arm,' I said. 'Call an ambulance.'

Cal followed my pointing finger to where Avery lay on the ground. He gasped, his hand flying to his mouth. I realised Cal must have rushed into the room so fast and acted so quickly that he hadn't even noticed his father, unconscious, on the floor.

In a flash, he crossed the room. He knelt down and touched Avery's cheek.

'Dad?' His voice cracked. '*Dad?*'

I turned back to Dylan. She was still holding Geri's gun, her eyes narrowed with determination.

'What are you doing?' I said.

'I'm going to kill Geri,' Dylan said steadily.

212

'Don't be stupid.' Geri's voice was as brisk and sharp-toned as ever, but – for the first time – she looked terrified.

'Please, Dylan,' Ed protested. 'Killing Geri won't solve anything. We've got the evidence that she murdered your dad. She'll be brought to justice and we can go home.'

'No.' Dylan shook her head so vigorously that her long, red ponytail whipped round her face. 'Geri will crawl out of it somehow. She always does. It won't matter who in the police we go to . . . she'll find some way to make sure what she's done gets covered up.'

'Not this time.' I rushed over to the computer and opened it up. 'I've got the confession here. Look.' I spun the computer round so that it was facing Dylan and Ed. 'You're right about Geri. She can stop investigations and smother evidence. But even Geri can't control the internet. Once her confession is out in public and online, nobody can hush it up.'

I bent down and clicked to upload the film onto YouTube. It was done.

Geri let out a furious snarl.

Dylan took a step back. 'Well, I'm still tying her up.'

'Be my guest.' I chucked Dylan the rope that had previously bound my own hands.

Dylan put down Geri's gun. As she fastened Geri's wrists, I glanced over at Avery. Cal was kneeling beside him now, his head in his hands.

'Cal,' I said sharply. 'Call your . . . our dad an ambulance.'

Cal looked up at me, clearly completely shell-shocked.

'Come on,' Ed said gently. 'I'll do it, but come with me to the phone. I don't know what 999 is in Australia.'

Cal got to his feet and followed Ed out of the room.

'I'm going to take Geri outside . . . tie her to the railings by the pool,' Dylan snarled, shoving Geri after Cal and Ed.

I stood for a second, alone, my pulse racing. Everything that could be done was being done.

A low moan from the other side of the coffee table reminded me that Ketty was still on the floor where Geri had pushed her down.

I raced over. Why hadn't she got up already? The answer was obvious as soon as I peered over the low table. The chair Ketty was tied to was too heavy for her to lift while her hands were still bound. Her face above the gag was red with the effort of trying to move it.

I reached out and teleported the rope off her wrists, then the gag from round her mouth. As they fell away, Ketty pushed herself up. It flickered across my mind that there was something different about the way she was holding herself. But I barely had time to think this before she had hurled herself across the short distance between us and was hugging me fiercely. As I held her, I felt a huge wave of emotion surge up through me.

'You're okay . . . you're okay . . .' I murmured.

Ketty turned her face up to mine and I was sure that whatever had happened, Ketty and I were cool again.

And I kissed her. Again I had the slight sense that something didn't feel the same as usual, but I was so happy I

214

didn't stop to think about it. I just kept my eyes squeezed shut, holding onto her for all I was worth, as the relief of knowing she was safe and that we were okay overwhelmed everything else.

'*Nico?*' It was Ketty's voice. And it appeared to be coming from the doorway several metres away.

Shocked, I leaped backwards, opening my eyes.

The girl in the doorway was definitely Ketty. She was staring at the girl I'd been kissing. I followed her gaze, my heart racing.

I couldn't believe my eyes.

'*Amy?*' I said. 'Is that *you*?'

26: Medutox

'Amy?' Ketty's shocked voice echoed my own.

I looked at the girl I'd been kissing. It was, indeed, Amy. As I watched, her face rounded out and her hair lengthened and straightened. I stared into her anxious eyes, feeling completely bewildered.

'Amy?' Ed said from the doorway of the Snug. 'What on earth are you doing here?'

'Geri brought me here,' Amy stammered desperately, her eyes fixing on her brother. 'She found out I'd taken her passport and impersonated her on the ferry. She kidnapped me back in England and forced me to show her my shape-shifting. Then she made me come with her here.'

'And Geri got you to shape-shift into Ketty?' I said.

'Yes.' Amy looked at the floor. 'She forced me to look like Ketty so that you'd be sure to do what she told you. She said I was her secret weapon.'

I glanced over at Ketty. Surely she would understand

my kissing Amy now? But Ketty avoided looking me in the eye.

'Geri and Dylan are outside,' she said. 'Cal's with them. He's called an ambulance for Avery. We need to keep him warm till they get here.'

'Okay.' I hurried over to Avery and knelt beside him. He was still unconscious. I touched his hand. Frozen.

'How long has it been since he was shot?' Ketty said.

'Just a few minutes,' I said. My heart felt like it was lodged in my throat. Surely I couldn't have just found my real father, only to lose him again within hours.

Behind us, Ed and Amy were talking in low voices. Amy was sobbing. As Ketty dragged a rug along the floor to cover Avery, I slipped a cushion under his head.

He moaned softly. At least that meant he was alive.

Ketty drew the rug over Avery. I caught her wrist as she turned away.

'I thought Amy was *you*,' I said. 'You have to believe I didn't know I was kissing her.'

Ketty met my eyes at last. Her expression was wary.

'It's more complicated than that,' she said.

I frowned. 'How?'

'I get that Amy was tied up before, but once you took the gag off her mouth, why didn't she explain it was her? Why didn't she change back straight away?'

'I don't know.'

'Because she *likes* you, that's why . . .' Ketty bit her lip.

217

'And what I'm asking myself is why Amy would think that she stood a chance with you.'

'What?' I couldn't properly follow what she was saying. 'Amy *doesn't* stand a chance with me. Man, she's a kid. And . . . and . . . I'm with *you*.'

'Are you?' Ketty narrowed her eyes.

I had no idea what she was getting at. But before I could even try and get my head round it, another gunshot rang out.

I was so preoccupied with worry over Avery and what Ketty was driving at that it took me a second to work out that the shot had come from outside – where Dylan had taken Geri. I glanced at the table where Dylan had laid Geri's gun. It was still there.

Did Geri have another hidden weapon?

I leaped to my feet. 'Dylan!' I rushed to the door, Ed right behind.

As we ran past the swimming pool, I could see Dylan and Cal in the distance. They were standing by the car that Geri, McMurdo and I had driven here in. Neither looked hurt.

Man, what on earth had happened?

We ran along the drive. Geri was visible now through the trees. She was bent over, staggering, clearly in agony. Cal and Dylan had their hands in the air as if in surrender. I frowned. That didn't make sense. Dylan's Medusa ability meant she didn't need to surrender to anyone. And why hadn't Cal flown away? What was going on?

And then another figure emerged from behind the car. McMurdo. Even from this distance, it was obvious that he was barely able to stand. His face was white as paint and contorted with pain. He advanced, limping, towards Dylan. The Medutox can dangled from his hand.

'I've shot Geri. I'm going to shoot you. I'll kill all of you.'

Ketty and I skidded to a halt. My heart pounded.

McMurdo must have sprayed Cal and Dylan with Medutox. They're completely vulnerable. I can't mind-read them remotely any more. Ed's thought-speech burst into my head.

Ketty clutched at my arm. 'I've seen this,' she said. 'Earlier. It didn't make sense, but now I see. McMurdo's going to shoot them.'

'No.' Fury swirled in my head. Geri had already shot my father. I wasn't going to let anyone hurt my brother or Dylan. 'I'll get the gun off him. Teleport him away.'

I turned back to McMurdo. He was right behind Cal now, his arm hooked round Cal's neck. I raised my hands.

Amy ran up. 'Wait,' she said breathlessly. 'He's too close. If you teleport McMurdo off the ground, he'll take Cal with him. I'll be you, Nico. Watch.'

'What?' Ed said.

But Amy was already changing. She grew taller, her face lengthening, her skin darkening.

'No,' Ed said.

Seconds later a mirror image of myself stood in front of me. It was one of the most bizarre sights of my life.

'What are you doing, Amy?' Ketty demanded.

'You don't have to—' I started.

But Amy was already tearing towards McMurdo, her arms waving in the air. 'Hey!' she yelled 'Wait!'

My pulse throbbed in my temple. I had to move. *Now.*

As McMurdo turned towards Amy, I ducked down, diving into the trees. The sudden coolness of the shade swept over me, clearing my head. I pounded through the woodland, keeping the edge of the trees close by. I emerged a few metres higher up and peered across to the car. Geri lay on the ground, motionless, next to the vehicle.

McMurdo still had a tight hold of Cal, who was struggling in vain to get away. Dylan stood beside them. McMurdo was pointing the Medutox can at Amy, but no spray came out. It was clearly empty. He threw it to the ground with a curse and raised his gun, pointing it at Amy.

She looked exactly like me. *Man*, that was weird.

'Stop or I shoot,' McMurdo yelled.

Nico? Ed made contact. His thought-speech was wild with panic. *Do something!*

Tell Cal to stop resisting, I ordered. *I need McMurdo to loosen his hold.*

I can't, Ed thought-spoke desperately. *He can't hear me. Nor can Dylan.*

Then tell Amy to drop to the ground. Now!

Ed's presence in my head vanished. I crept closer. I was behind McMurdo now. His gun was still pointing straight at Amy, his free arm still gripping Cal.

I reached out my hands. I was only going to get one chance at this.

Go! Ed's voice burst into my head.

As he spoke, Amy dropped to the ground. I turned to McMurdo. For a split second his attention left Cal as he focused on the version of me in front of him.

In a single movement, I raised McMurdo into the air, ripping the gun out of his hand. As I let him fall, I focused on Cal and Dylan and Amy, teleporting them in the opposite direction.

Swept off their feet, they landed in a heap close to Ed and Ketty.

I raced up to McMurdo, who had landed on his back at the end of the drive. He was lying, his body twisted and his eyes closed. With trembling fingers, I reached for his pulse.

Nothing. He was dead. This time definitely dead.

I straightened up and walked in a daze over to Geri.

She was lying on her side, her face twisted with pain.

I knelt down beside her. 'Geri?'

She gazed up at me. 'I didn't mean this to happen,' she whispered. 'All I ever wanted was the Medusa gene . . . to know that you are possible . . .' She closed her eyes. 'I didn't mean them all to die . . .'

The air seemed to grow still as I watched the life ebb out of her. I thought about all the people who had lost their lives because of the Medusa gene. My mother . . . all our mothers . . . and Dylan's dad, William Fox. And some of the people we'd met on missions, like McMurdo and poor Luz, the girl back in Spain.

And now Geri.

The others raced up. I could hear their feet pounding the dusty ground. We stood over Geri in a circle – all six of us – as she gave up a last sigh.

'Omigosh, is she dead?' Amy said in a timid whisper.

Ketty crouched down and reached for the pulse in Geri's neck. She looked up, nodding, as the blades of the emergency helicopter Cal had called for Avery whirred overhead.

I turned away, walking into my own shadow as the sun beat down. It was over.

We stayed at the ranch for another week. After a few uncomfortable hours in a Sydney police station giving statements, we finally got someone to call Fergus and Laura. They persuaded the police to take us back to Avery's ranch. Philly and Caro were already there with the children and insisted we stayed with them until Fergus and Ed's dad could fly out to take us home.

I had no problem with this. To be honest, I needed some time to let everything that had happened sink in. Avery was taken to hospital in Sydney. He had lost quite a lot of blood, but the bullet had passed cleanly through his arm and he was back home within forty-eight hours.

Fergus and Ed's dad arrived shortly afterwards and suddenly the house was full of adults asking questions.

Ed and Amy had a few questions, too. They immediately asked their father why he'd never revealed the truth that they were IVF.

'And the woman you used as a surrogate for Amy must have died after giving birth to her,' Ed said, nearly in tears. 'How could you and mum do that?'

'We didn't.' Ed's dad sighed. 'The surrogate for Amy was a cover. William Fox had started to have suspicions about Geri Paterson when you were conceived. He injected you both with the Medusa gene, but froze the Amy embryo in order to keep her secret. He didn't tell us about Medusa, but he warned us to keep Amy's identity hidden. Three years later we had to decide whether to let the embryo be destroyed or whether to let her develop inside the womb. Your mother was already ill, but she was determined to give Amy a chance of life. She carried her herself; there was no surrogate. That was a cover story, to protect Amy.'

While Ed and Amy were with their dad, I spent as much time as I could with Ketty – but there was a distance between us now which I didn't understand and didn't know what to do about.

Ketty said nothing about seeing Amy and me kissing again and we hung out like we always had, but it wasn't the same. I tried talking to Amy about it, too. I mean, I was really embarrassed that I'd told her I loved her, thinking she was Ketty, but why hadn't she identified herself when she'd had the chance?

If anything, Amy seemed even more humiliated by the whole incident than I was, so I dropped the subject.

The evening Fergus arrived, he and Avery took me to one side and confirmed again that neither of them had known – until Avery did the DNA test – that I was definitely Avery's son. They both seemed very concerned that I shouldn't be upset about the fact that I was discovering this so late in the day. I wasn't. Not once I understood how it had happened: Avery had left for Australia before my mum ever knew she was pregnant. Then, after Mum met Fergus, she decided it was best for me if she kept the true identity of my birth father secret. I guess she was trying to protect me. It certainly wasn't anyone else's fault that the truth had only just come out.

'It didn't even occur to me that you might be mine until I saw the classified MoD files last week,' Avery said. 'The truth is that I hardly knew Lucia. We only dated a few weeks. Plus, there's no obvious physical connection. You have your mother's dark colouring . . . all my other kids are blond, like *their* mums. I called Fergus when I found out because I wanted to talk to someone who knew you better than me about how to break the news.'

Fergus nodded his agreement. 'I was just taking an hour to work out what to say to you, but by the time I called back you'd gone.'

'You didn't show Ed any of this when he mind-read you,' I said to Avery. 'How did you manage that?'

Avery shrugged. 'I've done a lot of work on understanding

224

the way people's minds operate . . . a lot of work on my own mind. Holding stuff back from a telepath is just discipline.'

Another few days passed. Geri Paterson's death and the online confession that I'd posted on YouTube had, clearly, sent shockwaves through the British government. A team of representatives from London turned up to interview all six of us with the Medusa gene. They talked to us collectively and individually, asking for information and demonstrations of our powers.

It was clear that without Geri's confession we would have been totally screwed over Bookman's death. Geri had thoroughly framed us for that, using – as we'd suspected – the fact that we were angry at being manipulated to explain our motivation for the murder of the man behind the original medusa project.

After a few days the government agents went away to investigate further. We all knew they would be back before too long. They took with them McMurdo's computer, but not before Ed and I had managed to download a number of files. We'd been working our way through them and, so far, we'd found McMurdo's scientific formula for Medutox – and records of several suspicious-sounding meetings with various people referred to only by their initials.

Two more days passed. We played computer games and hung out by the pool. Dylan and Cal showed Ketty how to ride a horse. She loved it and spent all her waking hours from then on outdoors in the saddle.

I kept myself to myself. It's hard to explain, but seeing people die in front of you changes who you are. I used to think stuff like that was cool . . . exciting. Now I knew that it's mostly just shocking . . . and scary.

And then, one day, I found an item among McMurdo's files that shed a fierce beam of light on his recent work.

It was a secret journal of his attempts to create the drug that would replicate the power of the Medusa gene itself. The entry that caught my eye went like this:

> *I have destroyed the precise gene code formula which kills the mothers. But I'm still trying to use some of the threads of the code to create a drug that can confer the same abilities – Medusix. So far, all I've managed to do is accidentally develop a drug that I believe <u>inhibits</u> the actions of the gene – Medutox – but with renewed funding and help from my contact in Kima, I know Medusix will work.*

I showed the entry to everyone else when we met for dinner that evening. All of us with the Medusa gene were there – plus Fergus, Avery and Ed's dad.

'We need to find out who this contact of McMurdo's is,' I said. 'The journal entry was from four weeks ago; it says that the contact was helping to develop Medusix. We need to know if he has succeeded.'

Fergus cleared his throat. 'Actually, I think the best thing we can do is leave the investigations to the British

226

government.' He looked at me. 'We were going to tell you all tonight. We've agreed a new protection programme for you . . . Apart from anything else, you've missed far too much school work recently. The summer term is nearly halfway through and we need to get your education back on track as soon as possible.'

'What's a protection programme?' Amy asked.

'A new life, basically. The others have had to deal with all this happening before, but at least now the parents are in control,' Fergus said. He gazed round the table. 'We've agreed that Ed and Amy will go home. Their whole family will change their names and move to a different part of the country. Ketty will also change her name then be sent to a new boarding school. Dylan is coming with me to Scotland for a time while we work out how best to continue her education and keep her identity secret.'

'We're being split up?' I glanced at Ketty. She was avoiding my gaze. I turned to Fergus. 'What about me?'

He hesitated. 'Obviously, I want you with me, Nico,' he said heavily, 'but I have to accept that learning Avery is your birth father is a very big deal. So . . . it's up to you. You can come with me and Dylan now or you can stay here with Avery and Cal and your other half-brothers and -sisters for a while. I appreciate you have learned you have family you didn't know about. I don't want to stand in the way of you getting to know them.'

A tense silence filled the room. I looked around. How did the others feel about this?

'But we don't know if McMurdo's contact has managed to develop the Medusix,' Dylan protested.

'Imagine if they have,' Ketty said. 'They could be using it right now – in the place he mentions . . . Kima, wherever that is . . .'

'Which means there could be other people out there with Medusa skills,' Ed added.

'Like I said, the British government will investigate that,' Fergus said firmly.

'Yes,' Avery said. 'Our priority is keeping you safe, which means separating you and providing you with these new identities and new places to live so that no one – not the government nor any of the lowlifes who know of your existence – will find you.'

'No,' I said. 'We have a right to investigate what this contact in Kima has done with the Medusix drug ourselves.'

'Nico's right,' Ketty chipped in.

'We *have* to find out what's going on,' Dylan added.

'And make sure it's nothing bad,' said Ed.

Cal and Amy nodded their agreement.

Avery and Fergus looked at each other, clearly trying to work out how to convince us that we needed to do what they said. But in that moment I knew nothing they could say would make us accept being separated from one another and hidden away from the rest of the world

The tie that bound us was far greater than blood . . . bigger than either Fergus or Avery could ever imagine. We were a team . . . a family . . . Yes, Geri might be dead, but we were still the Medusa Project and our mission to use our skills to help others would not die until we did.

'We'll do what we need to do,' I said with a smile. 'Yeah, guys?'

And as I looked from face to face, I knew that there wouldn't be anything anyone could do to stop us.

More in . . . *Hit Squad*

Are you who you *think* you are?

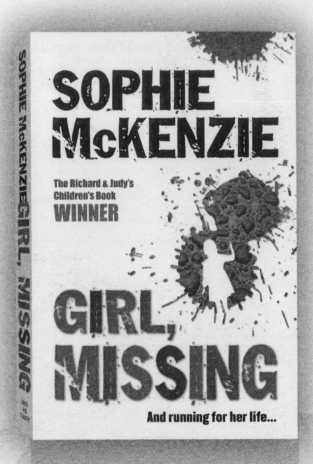

Lauren is adopted and eager to know about her mysterious past. But when she discovers she may have been snatched from another family as a baby, her whole life is turned upside down...

Could *you* be a clone?

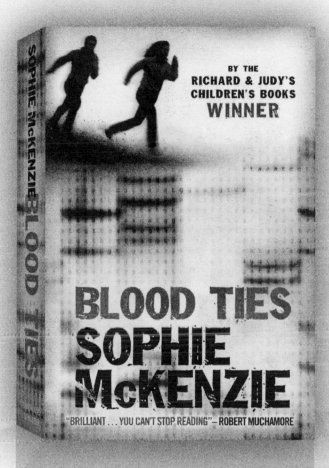

SOPHIE McKENZIE

BLOOD TIES

BY THE
RICHARD & JUDY'S
CHILDREN'S BOOKS
WINNER

BLOOD TIES
SOPHIE
McKENZIE

"BRILLIANT...YOU CAN'T STOP READING"– ROBERT MUCHAMORE

Linked by a firebombing at a research clinic,
Theo and Rachel fear they are targets of an
extremist group who will stop at nothing to
silence them - and who know more about
their true identities than they do . . .